THE LOCHVIEW MYSTERIES

The Trickster and the Thief

Ryan Vernel

The Lochview Mysteries:

The Lady of the Loch
The Trickster and the Thief

1

"Don't just stand there, you're going to make us late."

My sister Emily pushed me in the back, nudging me towards the iron gates of Caledonian Woods. It was our first day at our new school, and to be honest, it was a little bit terrifying. The building itself was huge, with grey stone walls and high arched windows. A spire-like clock tower loomed over us from its black slate roof.

"Are you coming or not?" she asked impatiently. "I'm not waiting for you."

I must have hesitated for a second too long, because the next thing I knew she was gone. Lost in a sea of green blazers.

"Wait!" I shouted, but it was too late.

There seemed to be an endless stream of people coming in from every direction. Some were dropped off in cars, some clambered off of packed busses, and others make their way along the main road.

I started moving forwards, but quickly found myself lost in the crowd. Surrounded by strangers on all sides, I started to get nervous. I had no idea where I was, and no idea where I was meant to be going.

Spotting a gap, I pushed through and freed myself from the hustle and bustle. I found a spot by some benches where I could see out across the playground.

Mum had told us over breakfast that Caledonian Woods used to be a Victorian poorhouse. A place where people were forced to live and work if they had no money and nowhere else to go.

Looking out at some of the faces walking past, I'm not sure much had changed.

Attached to the wall beside me was a large wooden notice board. On it was an assortment of coloured pages. But it was a crisp white poster in the bottom left corner that made the world around me stop.

Missing. Jackson Weir.

It had been almost a fortnight since my encounter with the Lady of the Loch, and even now I was still one of only a few people that knew Jackson's fate.

It was as I stood there, staring quietly at the poster, that I felt Kaya's hand on my shoulder. To say I was relieved to see a friendly face was an understatement. In fact, with Jackson gone, she was the only friendly face I could expect to find here, for now at least.

"You look lost," she said with a smile.

"Maybe a little," I admitted. "Where's the office?"

"I'll show you, follow me."

Before I even had a chance to reply, she grabbed me by the arm and started dragging me towards the main building. As we crossed the playground, she pointed at various parts of the building. "That's the Maths Block, English Block, Art, Music, then Geography is round the back—"

I tried my best to keep up, but she was speaking so quickly that I couldn't take it all in.

Her whirlwind tour paused briefly as we arrived at the large wooden reception desk. A tall dark-haired lady took my name and entered it into the computer in front of her. She squinted through the glasses perched on the end of her long sharp nose.

"Mrs Allen's class," she said.

"Thank you," Kaya chirped, gripping my arm once again. "This way, Tyler."

Without a pause for breath, we were back to the tour, twisting and turning through the school's maze of hallways. In a happy coincidence, it turned out Kaya was also in Mrs Allen's class.

When we got to the classroom for registration, I took a seat by Kaya. Everyone else was standing around or sitting on the tables. That was until precisely quarter to nine when the door opened and everyone hurriedly sat on their chairs.

I looked around nervously. How scary a teacher do you have to be to get that reaction when you enter a room?

But the woman who walked in didn't look scary at all.

Mrs Allan was an older lady, with grey curly hair and a multicoloured cardigan. Hardly the stuff of nightmares.

Then she opened her mouth.

"Silence!" she barked. Though I'm not sure anyone actually made a noise. "Let's get the register done and then I have some announcements for you all."

She rattled through the list of names like a sergeant major. Leaving barely enough time for people to respond.

"Tyler," she called.

"Here," I replied nervously.

"Welcome to Caledonian Woods," she said in a brief moment of warmth before she went back to her roll call.

Whilst she was talking something weird caught my eye. Out the window, I saw a small deer strolling boldly across the playground. I'll admit I was still getting used to living in Scotland, but I was sure that couldn't be normal.

"Are you still with us, Tyler?" Mrs Allen stood with her arms crossed.

"Yes, Miss, sorry," I bumbled. "I just thought I saw—"

"Thought you saw what?"

I looked back, but the playground was empty.

"Nothing, Miss," I answered, embarrassed.

4

Ring!

Saved by the bell.

In a wave of movement, everyone stood from their chairs. They all grabbed their bags and coats and made their way to the door.

"Before you go," Mrs Allen shouted above the noise. "Preparations for the festival this weekend are underway. Please take a letter as you leave and fill in the slip at the bottom if you wish to volunteer."

As the class filtered out, a small blonde girl in front of me turned to her friend.

"Volunteer?" She laughed. "Do I look like the kind of person who volunteers?"

She took a letter from Mrs Allen and made a point of screwing it up into a tight ball, before throwing it over her shoulder into the crowded hallway.

"That is Verity Gowers," Kaya said under her breath. "If I was you, I'd steer clear."

"Noted," I replied, taking a letter.

"What have you got first?" Kaya asked, hovering in the doorway.

I pulled a small timetable out of my pocket.

"Science, I think." I held it out to her so she could double-check.

"Perfect," she smiled. "This way."

We pushed out into the mob of people filling the halls. Dodging and weaving through pupils, teachers and the occasional rogue football, I glanced down at the letter I'd just received.

"What's the Rowan Festival?" I shouted to Kaya, struggling to keep up.

"It's this thing in town," she called back. "There's music, and stalls, and games, and stuff. It's actually alright, to be fair."

"Sounds cool," I replied. "What's it for?"

For a moment she didn't reply, and I was starting to think she hadn't heard me.

"Kaya?" I tapped her on the shoulder and she stopped.

"It's just a silly little festival thing." She shrugged awkwardly, but I could tell there was something she wasn't telling me. "It's nothing interesting, it all revolves around some story about these trees—"

"Hang on," I interrupted. "Did you say trees?"

"The trees are said to protect the town."

She suddenly had my interest. The warm buzz of excitement started flowing through my veins.

"Protect it from what?" I asked.

She hesitated again.

"You're going to think it's crazy."

I was confused. I'd met Kaya whilst searching for a child-snatching ghost. What could possibly be crazier than that?

"No, I won't," I said. "Come on, tell me."

She stared at me for a moment then sighed.

"OK, but you have to promise not to laugh."

2

"Fairies?" I asked, for about the hundredth time.

"Fair Folk," Kaya corrected, shuffling forward in the lunch queue. "Either that or Fae, but definitely not Fairies."

"Sorry, I wouldn't want to offend them," I joked. "What are they going to do? Sprinkle me in magic dust?"

I'd had a whole morning of lessons since Kaya explained the festival to me, and still it felt totally insane.

It starts with the cutting of a branch from the Rowan Trees on the edge of Lochview. The branch is then walked through the streets in an attempt to ward off any evil fairies. Then, after a good hour of fighting imaginary things with a big stick, it's dumped in the middle of town. Where there are loads of stalls, food and music.

I couldn't help but laugh.

It was ridiculous.

"If you'd told me a month ago that ghosts were real, I'd have said you were crazy." Kaya placed her tray on an empty table and sat down. "We both know how that turned out."

"Yeah, but that's ghosts," I argued sitting opposite her. "If you gave me the choice between fighting a ghost or some cute little Fairy, then I am grabbing my flyswatter and I am squashing that glittery little bug."

I slammed my hand down on the table sending a spiral of pasta tumbling from Kaya's plate.

She did not look happy.

"Hang on a minute." I could feel the smile spreading across my lips. "Kaya, do you believe in fairies?"

"That's not what I'm saying," she replied, a little too forcefully. "I just think that if we know ghosts exist, then maybe we shouldn't be so quick to say that Fae don't."

With that she took a victorious bite of her lunch.

"You should listen to her," said a quiet voice behind me.

I looked over my shoulder, but all I saw was the packed lunch hall. It was just table after table of students laughing and joking, entirely unaware that I even existed, let alone trying to talk to me.

"Are you guys into ghosts and stuff?"

I nearly jumped out of my skin. Seemingly out of nowhere, a boy had pulled a chair up to the table and was now grinning excitedly. He flicked his sweeping black fringe out of his face, it had a bold red streak that seemed to almost glow in the light.

I looked at Kaya, a little lost for words.

"We were just talking hypothetically," she said, smiling awkwardly back at him. "Like, if people believe ghosts are real, why shouldn't they believe fairies are real?"

"Fae," the boy corrected, much to Kaya's frustration.

"Yes, that's what I meant," she fumbled. "Why shouldn't they believe Fae are real?"

"Exactly." He nodded. "Because they are. I've seen proof."

Kaya looked back at him confused, so I tried to step in.

"Sorry, I don't think we've met yet," I said. "I'm Tyler."

"Oh, you must be the new kid." Pulling back the long sleeve of the black hoody he was wearing under his blazer, he held out his hand towards me. "I'm Abdirahman. Though my friends call me Absy."

I looked past his smiling face at the empty table behind him.

"OK, my cousins call me Absy," he laughed. "But if I had friends, they would too."

As I looked at him my mind thought back to Jackson, a loner kid with a love of the supernatural, they were like peas in a pod.

"Do you guys mind if I sit here?" He asked, grabbing his tray.

"Yes," Kaya mumbled under her breath.

"No," I said loudly, shooting her a look.

"Thanks." He placed his food next to mine on the table and took a seat. "Have you been to The Beyond yet?"

"The Beyond?" I repeated.

"It's a weird little shop in town. They sell all these horrible gross things that are meant to be dark and magical," Kaya explained.

"It's amazing," Absy beamed. "If you're into the supernatural, then you have to go there. Mr McPhee, the guy who owns it, has a real-life boggart fang."

"What's a boggart?" I asked.

"What's a boggart?" he repeated. His eyes lit up with excitement. "A boggart is a shapeshifting Fae that can transform into any animal or human. It's incredibly rare to see one in its true form. But if you do, they are said to have long, razor-sharp fangs, strong enough to rip your arm clean off."

Kaya looked at me, it was clear from her face that she wanted nothing more than for the conversation to end. But I thought it was kind of cool, Absy seemed fun.

"We could head into town after school if you want?" he offered. "I could show you around the shop."

"I don't think—" Kaya started.

"Sounds great," I interrupted, talking over her.

"Brilliant, I'll meet you at the gates after the bell." He smiled widely, grabbing his tray and rising from the seat.

When he turned to walk away, Kaya kicked me under the table.

"What did you do that for?" She snarled.

"What do you mean?" I winced as I rubbed my shin.

"I don't want to go to —" She paused, lowering her voice. "That place."

"The Beyond?"

"Don't say it out loud," she snapped. "People might hear you."

"What is so bad about The Beyond?" I asked.

"It's creepy," she replied with a shudder. "I don't like the thought of it."

"OK, well no one is forcing you to come along," I shrugged. "But if you don't, then I guess you'll never know for sure."

"Know what for sure?" She looked at me confused.

I crossed my arms with a smile.

"You'll never know if fairies really do exist."

3

A sharp ring of the bell signalled the end of the day. In a flurry of movement and noise, the entire school flooded out towards the main gate.

"Do you really want to go to The Beyond with Absy?" Kaya asked as we followed the crowds.

"Why not?" I shrugged. "It sounds like it could be cool."

"It's weird and it's creepy," she replied.

I stopped in my tracks and looked at her.

"Are you scared of The Beyond?"

Kaya shifted uncomfortably and carried on walking.

"You are scared." I couldn't help but smile. "What is it, Kaya? Is it the thought of the Fairies coming to get you?"

"I'm not scared!" she said a little too forcefully. "I just don't see what the big deal is. A shop full of skulls and bones and gruesome things, why is that so exciting to you? It's probably all fake anyway."

"Not with Mr McPhee's Guarantee." Absy suddenly appeared between us, wrapping his arms around our shoulders. "One hundred percent genuine Fae, or your money back. Though you would of course have to prove it's not real, which I guess is easier said than done."

He grinned widely, looking from me to Kaya and back again. I smiled in return, but Kaya shrugged free of his arm and started walking off ahead.

"What's wrong with her?" he asked, under his breath.

"I don't know," I replied.

Something felt wrong. Kaya seemed so sensible and down to earth, but all this fairy stuff seemed to really unnerve her.

It was roughly a forty-minute walk into town from Caledonian Woods. Luckily for us, the sun was shining and there was barely a cloud in the sky. It was even warm enough to melt the cold shoulder Kaya had been giving us since we left.

Before long we were all laughing and joking as we took a shortcut through the fields. A herd of Highland Cows stood and watched as we passed by, their long ginger hair hanging over their eyes.

"Don't you think they look like punk rock cows?" Absy asked us. As he climbed the stile at the other end of the field, he turned back and held up his hand in a rocker's salute. "Rock on, you hairy beasts!"

Absy was definitely growing on me, there was no doubt he was crazy, but he was also pretty fun. It was kind of infectious. Even Kaya couldn't help but smile when he decided to tell us his top ten reasons for wanting a pet goat.

Three of which involved very specific types of headbutts.

Finally, Lochview came into view on the horizon. Beyond the rows of shops and houses, I could see the waters of Loch Dowell shimmering in the sunlight.

Absy led us down to the high street. We strolled past the charity shops and antique stores until we reached a stone arch. With an eager grin, he stepped through, into a dark and narrow alleyway.

There was a chill in the air as we followed the rough cobblestones that wound around the back of the shops. Finally, they came to an end at a staircase leading down beneath the ground.

"I can't wait for the two of you to see this place," Absy said, a twinkle in his eye. "You're going to love it, I can tell."

I had to admire his confidence, but there was a nervousness beginning to churn in the pit of my stomach.

"The two of you should go ahead without me," Kaya said. "I should really be getting home anyway."

"No don't." I grabbed her arm in a moment of panic. "I mean, we'll just take a quick look. Two minutes and then we're out of there."

"Two minutes?" she confirmed.

I nodded, letting go of her arm.

"OK."

I looked down to see Absy standing patiently by a crooked wooden door, its frosted glass concealing what lay on the other side.

"Well come on then," he called up to us. "What are you waiting for?"

There was a soft chime of a bell as he pushed open the door and stepped inside. Both me and Kaya hesitated a moment before making our way down the stairs. As we reached the bottom we were greeted by a small wooden sign above the doorway.

Welcome to The Beyond. Emporium of Dark Obscurities.

The smell hit me first.

The stale air was thick with dust and scented smoke. I coughed as it scratched the back of my throat.

It took a few moments for my eyes to adjust to the darkness of the shop, but when they did, I couldn't believe what I was seeing. Despite its small size, every single inch, from rough stone wall to rough stone wall, was put to use.

Cupboards and cabinets filled every nook and cranny. That was if they weren't already occupied by a table or shelves. Each surface was laden with dark and sinister trinkets.

"You first," Kaya whispered, pushing me in the back.

Cautiously I took a step forward, the wooden floorboards creaking beneath my feet. To my right was a stack of shelves, filled with long lines of large glass jars. It was like some kind of nightmare fuelled sweet shop. Though instead of cola bottles and gummy snakes, there were twisted roots and slimy tentacles. At the end of the row stood a jar, full to the brim with thick black ink-like fluid. Wiping away the dust, I tapped gently on the glass. As the dark liquid rippled a small round object floated to the surface.

Why is there an eyeball in a jar?!

My stomach turned. It took all my strength not to throw up there and then.

"You must be Tyler," came a slow breathless voice.

I turned to see a small old man limping towards me.

"And this is Kaya," Absy added, following a step behind.

The man stared at her for a moment, before giving a small nod.

"I am Mr McPhee," he wheezed, "and this is The Beyond."

His wrinkled face twisted into a crooked smile.

With his bulbous nose, thin white hair, and hunched back, Mr McPhee reminded me of a goblin, or maybe some kind of troll. All I could say for certain was, in the dim light of the shop, he looked more like a creature than a man.

"How may I be of assistance today?" He asked, looking expectantly between the three of us.

"We were hoping you could tell us about Fair—"

He grabbed my wrist surprisingly hard, stopping me mid-sentence.

"Careful," he warned, leaning in so close I could feel his warm breath on my face. "That is not a word we use. You never know who is listening, especially in here."

He tapped the side of his nose and gave me a knowing nod. Nervously I nodded back, his lips curled into a small wry smile.

"The Fae are both conniving and resourceful, they are often listening when you least expect it." He glanced over his shoulder. "People will often tell you about the cute little magical creatures roaming the Highlands, but I know better."

He gestured for us to follow as he turned and led us deeper into the shop.

"Fae is a collective term for many different species, all of which are enhanced with supernatural abilities," he explained. "Make no mistake, they could bring down our world with just a click of their fingers. That is why we must be ready to defend ourselves."

Mr McPhee raised a bony finger to the ceiling. Above us, an assortment of vicious-looking traps and cages hung from thick rusty chains. Each was constructed from pieces of jaggedly cut metal.

"That's barbaric," Kaya said quietly.

"That is war," McPhee shot back. "Of course, these will only do for the little ones. The bigger ones require a little more cunning and creativity."

I was starting to feel queasy again.

It was one thing for Mr McPhee to think that the Fae were dangerous, but I was beginning to think he actually enjoyed the thought of hunting them. Proudly he started to show off his collection. There were tiny winged skeletons preserved in glass, curved horns hollowed into cups, and windchimes made from tiny bones. These all used to be living things, and now he sells them as if they are souvenirs from a trip to The Beyond.

Whether they were real or not didn't matter. The Fae were real enough to him, and all he wanted to do was destroy them.

I could see from the horror on Kaya's face that she felt the same as me. I looked back towards Absy, but he was gone.

"Guys, you have got to see this," came a voice from a dark corner of the shop.

We cut between two rows of shelves to find Absy standing with a small wooden box. Its dark stained lid rested open, revealing an ancient treasure inside.

Gold coins.

Absy turned one over in his finger as the biggest of smiles spread across his face.

"Put that back!" McPhee cried. Slamming the box shut. "Do you even realise what you could have done, you foolish boy?!"

"I'm sorry, I—" he stuttered.

The old man snatched the box and tucked it under his arm. With a cold glare, he turned and limped away, mumbling as he slinked off into the darkness.

Before he vanished from view he paused. Without even turning around he called back to us.

"You should all go home. The shop is closed until further notice."

"But Mr McPhee—" Absy started.

He raised his hand cutting Absy off.

"I would like you all to leave."

5

"I was only taking a look," Absy protested as we climbed the stairs back to street level. "It's a shop, that's what people in a shop do."

The door slammed shut behind us.

"I'm just happy to be out of there," Kaya said with a shudder. "If I've said it once, I've said it a thousand times, that place gives me the creeps."

"In a good way, right?" Absy somehow looked surprised that she wasn't a fan. "It's like a fun kind of creepy."

"Let me put it this way, if either of you try to make me step foot in that shop again, we are no longer friends."

She marched past the two of us, heading back to the main road.

"Wait a minute," Absy called after her. "Does that mean we're friends?"

"You're alright I guess," she replied, disappearing round the corner.

We followed after her, catching up as she stepped onto the high street.

"Tyler!"

My dad's voice caught me off guard. I spun around to see him standing by the car across the street. His hands were on his hips and his eyes were wide.

I was in trouble.

"Where have you been?" he shouted as he crossed towards me. "I've been looking everywhere for you."

Suddenly it hit me. Mum told me this morning that I was to wait for Emily after school and head back with her. I'd totally forgotten.

"Well, I waited for Emily, but I couldn't—"

"Don't do it," he interrupted. "Right now, I'm annoyed, but if you try to lie to me, I'm going to get angry."

I hated when he did that. It was like he was telling you off before you'd even done what he was telling you off for.

"We should get going," Kaya said awkwardly, shuffling backwards. "We'll see tomorrow."

"Yeah, I'll see you at school," I replied.

"Get in the car," Dad ordered. Based on the vein throbbing on the side of his head, he was more than annoyed. "Did you not even think to call? What is the point in you having a phone if you're not going to answer it."

As I pulled my mobile out of my pocket the screen lit up to show nine missed calls.

"It was still on silent from school," I explained, but Dad just shook his head.

I climbed into the backseat. For a moment we sat in silence. Then Dad let out a sigh.

"You had us really worried, Tyler," he said. "I know you're getting older, and it might not be the coolest thing in the world to have to walk home with your big sister. Just have a little more thought next time. Anything could have happened to you, and we'd never have known."

"I'm sorry," I mumbled.

He was talking to me like a child, and I hated it. I was only walking home, what's the big problem? If he knew half the things I'd seen since we'd moved to Lochview it would blow his mind.

But it wasn't worth the argument.

"Your friends seem nice at least." He tried a softer tone. I could see him looking back at me in the rear-view mirror. "Come on, we'll pick your mum and sister up on the way home, they waited at the café in case you went there."

Dad shifted the car into gear and drove us down a little side road, before pulling up on the curb outside his and Mum's pride and joy.

Their beloved Café.

It had come a long way in the last couple of weeks. It had new windows, a new door, and the once empty interior had been repainted and filled with chairs and tables. The toilets still didn't flush and the heating wasn't working, but it was definitely getting closer to being ready for its grand opening.

Outside, Mum was pacing up and down the pavement, and Emily sat perched in the doorway.

"Don't panic," Dad announced, lowering his window. "The wanderer has returned."

"Thank goodness," Mum said with a sigh of relief. "Where was he?"

"Up on the high street," Dad replied.

The two of them continued as if I wasn't even there for the whole drive home. Back and forward about how I should have called, and how anything could have happened. Meanwhile, my sister sat subtly smirking, loving every minute of the drama.

Even when we got home they were still going. It was relentless.

By the time we sat down for dinner, I was exhausted. There is only so many times you can nod along to the same conversation before it wears you out.

"You feeling alright, Tyler?" Mum asked.

I'd been stabbing at the same stubborn pea for the last five minutes.

"I'm not very hungry," I replied, laying down my knife and fork. "I might just go to bed."

"Oh, OK then." Mum gave a concerned look in Dad's direction. "Do you want me to bring you anything?"

"No, I'm fine."

My chair scratched on the tiled floor as I stood up. I could feel their eyes on me as I headed for the stairs, but I didn't care. I just wanted to be in my room, behind a closed door, where no one was there to remind me I was just a kid.

6

I turned off the light and climbed into bed. I wanted to bury my face in the pillow and scream.

It wasn't fair.

Emily was only a couple of years older than me, so why can she do whatever she wants?

All I did was walk home with my friends, but everyone is acting like I'd run away to Timbuktu.

It was ridiculous, and it was unfair.

There's no point arguing though, they'd tell I'm being childish. They'd say that I'm proving them right.

I closed my eyes, hoping that sleep would come quickly. I just wanted this day to be over. More than anything I wanted to be anywhere that my family wasn't.

If only Lochview had a bus to Timbuktu.

As I began to drift off the sounds and smells of my room faded away, replaced by something strange yet familiar. It was the burning incense that hit me first, hanging thick in dust-filled air.

I was in The Beyond.

It was crazy, I knew I was asleep yet everything felt so real. From the rough texture of the wooden shelves to the gentle creak of the floorboards beneath my feet. It was like I was there.

At the far end I saw Mr McPhee sitting at the counter, his eyes wide and his mouth stretched into an evil grin. A cold chill crept up the back of my neck.

"Mr McPhee?" I called.

There was no reply, he didn't even move.

I took a step towards him.

Buzz!

It was faint, but it was definitely there. It sounded like the hum of electricity. It was like everything in the room was gently vibrating.

I scanned across the room, looking for the source of the noise, but it was no use. I was looking for something out of the ordinary, in a shop that only sells things that are out of the ordinary.

Turning back to Mr McPhee, my heart sank.

He was gone.

I started backing away towards the door. I could feel the nerves beginning to swirl in the pit of my stomach.

Suddenly I stopped. I could feel a presence behind me. There was someone standing between me and the door.

I tried to turn around but I couldn't. My fear left me frozen to the spot.

I heard the soft groan of the floorboards behind me, as a deep and menacing laughter filled the air.

I sat up in bed. My covers were drenched in sweat.

It was just a nightmare.

I rubbed my eyes and reached for my bedside lamp. I was about to flick the switch, but something stopped me.

Dark as it might have been, I knew I was in my room. There was just enough moonlight coming in around the curtains for me to see that. So, I knew for a fact that what I had seen was all in my head. A simple figment of my imagination.

Yet, I could still hear the buzzing.

With a soft click, the lamp lit up the room. Everything was exactly how I'd left it, or at least nothing looked to be out of place.

I climbed out of bed, listening carefully, again trying to find where it was coming from. Pressing my ear against my bedroom door I heard nothing. It wasn't coming from inside the house.

I crept back across the room to the window.

Even though the moon wasn't quite full, it still shone bright enough to illuminate the Loch. The water rippled gently as it lapped against the shore. The trees swayed softly in the wind.

The window jammed as I pushed against the handle. I looked back over my shoulder, hoping the rest of the house were sound asleep. Then I put all my weight into giving it a shove.

It burst free, almost sending me headfirst through the open gap. I fumbled wildly to catch it before it swung back against the wall.

The buzzing sound carried towards me on the ice-cold winds, but try as I might, I couldn't see where it was coming from.

Scanning over the hills and the fields there was nothing.

It was just darkness.

And it seemed to be getting darker.

Ominous clouds rolled over the sky, gradually blocking the light from the moon. They looked thick and menacing, and moved far quicker than anything I'd ever seen before.

The soft pitter-patter of rain spread slowly towards me. Starting gently at first before getting heavier and heavier.

As the rain built, so did the buzzing. Getting louder and louder until it was almost unbearable.

Crack!

A bolt of lightning ripped through the sky. It looked almost purple in colour, as it carved through the clouds.

Moments later a deep rumble of thunder filled the air. Then the buzzing started to build again.

Crack! Crack!

There was no doubt about it, this storm was big.

Yet somehow no one had seen it coming.

There had been no talk of a storm on the news. Not so much as a mention of rain in the weather report.

Which was strange in itself, because it was always raining up here.

I closed the window and fell back into bed.

It was going to be a long night.

7

"Thunderbugs," Absy said confidently, around a mouth full of chips.

"Thunder-whats?" I replied.

"The buzzing was probably Thunderbugs," he explained. "They can sense the electricity in the air before a storm. It drives them crazy, makes them fly about."

"Oh, right," I mumbled, feeling dumb. "Do you not think it's a little weird though? The storm came out of nowhere."

"It's Lochview," Kaya shrugged. "It rains. You're going to have to get used to it."

They both chuckled, but it didn't put me at ease. Something was still churning away in the pit of my stomach. The speed at which the storm started, the purple tinge to the lightning, the volume of the buzzing, it wasn't natural.

It couldn't be.

31

Not that the two of them seemed to care. When I'd mentioned it to Kaya that morning in registration, she just stared at me blankly. Apparently, she'd slept through the whole thing.

Absy said the same when we saw him before English.

Now we were sitting in the lunch hall and even I was starting to doubt if it had actually happened.

"Changing the subject," Absy said, slamming his hands down on the table. "You guys want to see something cool?"

I glanced at Kaya, she looked just as surprised and confused as I was.

"Yeah, sure," I replied.

Absy reached excitedly into his blazer pocket. He rummaged for a minute, then pulled out a small gold coin.

"What is that?"

Verity Gowers emerged from the crowd of students hovering by the tables. Before he had a chance to answer, she snatched the coin from his hands, turning it over in her fingers.

"Hey, give that back," Absy demanded, but she didn't listen.

"Well it's obviously not real," she laughed. "Is it some nerd thing? Are you all planning a pirate party or something?"

A group of girls gathered around her, cackling like a pack of hyenas.

"Oh wait." An evil grin spread across her face. "If you were going to throw a party, you'd actually need friends."

She tossed the coin in the air, and Absy snatched at it wildly.

The girls moved on with a chorus of cruel taunts and laughter.

"Hey, are you OK?" I asked.

Absy gripped the coin so tight, his knuckles were turning white.

"I'm fine," he replied through gritted teeth. His eyes locked angrily on Verity as she walked away.

"Absy, where did you get that?" Kaya asked.

"It doesn't matter."

"Actually, I think it does," she said, glancing at me. "Because that looks a lot like the coins that were in the box at The Beyond."

Something changed in his expression, he looked sheepishly between the two of us.

"I need to go."

"Did you steal that?" Kaya asked, lowering her voice.

"It's none of your business." He stood from his seat and grabbed his bag.

"Come on, Absy," she sighed. "I wish you'd just tell us the truth."

"Yeah, well I wish Verity would go and eat worms," he snapped back. "But I guess we don't always get what we wish for."

He turned to walk away but hadn't even made it ten paces before an ear-splitting scream rang through the hall. Everyone stopped and turned toward the double doors that opened onto the back fields.

For the briefest of moments, everything was silent and still. Then like a stampede on the Serengeti, the sea of students burst towards the open doors.

Teachers tried telling people to slow down, but no one was listening.

The scream rang out again as an excited chatter started to build.

I looked at Kaya, and she looked back.

There was no way we were missing this.

We grabbed our bags and followed everyone out into the cold fresh air.

"Verity, stop!" said a panicked voice.

I froze.

What could Verity possibly be doing to make someone scream like that?

I pushed my way to the front, dragging Kaya along behind me. When I finally burst free from the crowd my stomach turned.

Verity was crawling on the ground, pulling up chunks of mud with her bare hands. Suddenly, she stopped. Reaching into the small hole she had made, she pulled out a long thick worm.

"Is she—" Kaya started, but she got her answer before she could finish the question.

Eyes wide with terror, Verity took the wriggly pink bug and lowered it slowly into her mouth.

"I think I'm going to be sick," said a voice behind us in the crowd.

I could see tears roll down Verity's cheek as she began to chew.

"Verity, please stop," cried one of her friends.

"V, what are you doing?" bawled another.

"No way!"

I turned to see Absy standing next to me, a wide grin on his face.

Kaya grabbed his arm.

"You need to stop this," she whispered forcefully in his ear.

"What are you talking about?" he replied. "I'm not doing anything."

"You wished that Verity would go and eat worms," Kaya argued, "and now she is chowing down in the soil. There is no way that is a coincidence."

"Yeah, I said it." Absy broke free of her grip. "But I'm not making her do this."

The two of them stared angrily at each other. Verity meanwhile started digging around for another snack.

That was when it hit me.

"The coin."

"What?" Absy and Kaya replied in unison.

"You were holding the coin when you said it," I continued. "What if it has some kind of power?"

"That's ridiculous," Absy said, looking at me as if I was mad.

"Mr McPhee did get pretty angry when you opened that box," Kaya shrugged.

Absy stood for a moment, then when he realised he wasn't going to win, he reached into his pocket.

"OK fine, but don't blame me if it doesn't work," he grumbled. "I wish Verity would stop eating worms."

There was silence. No screaming, no gossiping, nothing at all. Verity knelt frozen to the spot as everyone watched in anticipation.

"I think it worked," I whispered.

"Are you OK, Verity?" asked her friend, placing a hand on her shoulder.

Verity looked up towards her.

Then clutched her hand across her mouth and sprinted towards the toilets.

Chatter erupted once more as everyone dispersed.

Before long it was only the three of us left.

Absy held out the coin in the palm of his hand, a mixture of fear and excitement in his eyes.

"Do you realise what this means?" he beamed. "Whatever we want, it's ours. It's magic, the coin is actually magic."

Kaya wasn't convinced, she started telling him that it could be dangerous, but I had stopped listening.

Whilst the two of them were bickering, I had seen something out of the corner of my eye. Or at least I thought I'd seen something.

It was nothing more than a shadow.

A shadow stood at the window on the second floor.

A shadow stood watching us down below.

8

"You two need to stop," I said, stepping between Kaya and Absy. "Look up there."

They both turned their heads in the direction I was pointing, but there was nothing to be seen.

The mysterious figure had vanished.

"What are we meant to be looking at?" Kaya asked.

"There was someone there," I replied defensively. "They were watching from the window."

"Verity Gowers just ate worms," Absy pointed out. "The whole school was watching."

"What did they look like?" Kaya continued, ignoring him.

"I don't know," I said. "It was more like a shadow."

"Well, they're not there now," Absy shrugged. He dipped his hand into his pocket and pulled out the coin. "Now, who wants to make the next wish?"

"No way." Kaya snatched the coin from his hand.

"Hey, give that back," he yelled. "It's mine!"

"No it's not," she corrected. "You stole it."

"Yeah, well finders keepers."

"And losers weepers," she countered smugly.

Absy turned to me, a look of desperation on his face.

"Come on, Tyler," he pleaded. "Tell her she's being boring."

I thought back to our visit to The Beyond. In particular, I thought back to how suddenly it ended.

"Mr McPhee did seem pretty angry that you opened that box," I said. "What if it's dangerous?"

"Think about it," Absy groaned in frustration. "He wasn't angry because it was dangerous, he was angry because we just discovered his real-life magic coins. He wanted to keep them all for himself, keep them as his little secret."

I looked at Kaya, he could be right for all we knew.

"Are you really saying there is nothing you want?" I could feel his eyes locked on me. "Just one little wish, Tyler. What's the worst that could happen?"

As crazy as it sounds, I was tempted. Anything in the world, I just had to say the word and it was mine.

It was kind of exciting.

"Why are the three of you not in class?"

Mrs Allen's dulcet tones drifted across the empty playground. I glanced at my watch. In all the commotion we'd missed the bell.

"Sorry, Miss," Kaya stuttered, "we must have lost track of time."

"Yeah, sorry," Absy added, "we'll head there straight away."

"No you won't," she replied, crossing her arms. "You'll follow me to the headteacher's office."

She turned and headed back inside.

We all glanced at each other nervously.

"I've not got all day," she called back through the open door.

We walked in silence, scared to make even the slightest of sounds. The corridors felt weirdly empty when everyone else was in class.

My stomach sank as she led us into reception. It was only my second day at Caledonian Woods, and I was already being sent to the head. If my parents found out, they would ground me for the rest of time. Even longer if they could.

"Take a seat," Mrs Allen instructed, pointing to a row of blue chairs by the wall.

We did as we were told.

She went to the desk and spoke to the receptionist in hushed tones. After a short discussion, she gave the receptionist a small nod and turned back to us.

"Mr Schaeffer will see you in a minute," she said. "He will come and get you when he is ready."

With that, she left.

We sat and waited in silence. There was nothing but the sound of the clock ticking on the wall and the soft click-clack of the receptionist's keyboard.

"We should get out of here," Absy whispered under his breath.

"And how do you suggest we do that?" Kaya bit back.

"Oh, I don't know," he replied. "If only we had some kind of magical coin that makes wishes come true."

"Are you actually crazy?" I could hear the anger swelling in her voice.

"Tyler, back me up here."

They were both looking at me, waiting for an answer.

I hesitated, then turned to Kaya.

"I'm already in trouble with my parents after yesterday," I said. "If they find out I've been skipping class, they're going to hit the roof."

"But we weren't skipping class," Kaya argued.

"Do you really think they're going to believe that?" Absy folded his arms as he sat back with a hint of a smile. He knew he'd won.

Reluctantly, Kaya reached into her pocket, pulled out the coin and slipped it into my hand.

"This is a mistake."

Deep down, I think I knew that was true, but what other choice did we have?

"What do I say?" I asked, looking to the two of them for help.

"Just make a wish," Absy replied with a shrug. "That's what I did."

"OK." I paused, trying desperately to find the right words. "I wish we could get out of here."

9

The world stood still.

Not in a metaphorical way. It literally stood still. The clock stopped ticking on the wall, the receptionist froze behind her desk, even the birds outside the window hung motionless in the sky.

"Tyler," Kaya said nervously. "What did you do?"

"I didn't do anything," I replied. "I just said I wanted to get out of here."

Absy climbed to his feet and walked cautiously to the reception desk.

"This is crazy," he said, waving his hand in front of the receptionist's face. She didn't even flinch.

"Stop that!" Kaya growled.

"I think you stopped time." Absy's eyes lit up.

"But how?" I asked, still completely lost.

"Well, what better way to get out of here?" he shrugged. "It's not like anyone can stop us."

There was a spring in his step as he headed for the door.

"What are you doing?" Kaya said, grabbing his arm.

"I'm leaving," he replied. "Tyler wished for us to get out of here, so let's get out of here."

"No." She placed herself between Absy and the door. "We should stay here. Whatever this is, we should unwish it."

"Unwish it?" he laughed. "If we stay here, we're going to get in trouble. The whole point of making the wish was to avoid that. So, I'm going to go. Tyler, are you coming?"

I could feel their eyes burning into me.

There was a real fear on Kaya's face, and I could understand why. We didn't know what this coin was, not really. We knew it grants wishes, but was that all? What if it was dangerous? Mr McPhee seemed to think it was.

But then again, Absy was right. I couldn't risk getting in trouble again, that was why I made the wish.

"It's already done," I said, looking apologetically at Kaya. "There's no point going back on it now."

"That's two against one," Absy announced. "So, are you staying here on your own, or are you coming with us?"

Kaya folded her arms.

"You better hope that nothing bad happens," she said. "Otherwise, I will never let you forget that I told you this was a bad idea."

She stepped aside, and Absy pressed the button to open the front door.

Nothing happened.

He tried it again, and again, and again.

"It's an electric door," Kaya said.

"Yeah, and?" Absy snapped.

"If everything in the world is frozen, then how is the motor going to move?"

He opened his mouth, then shut it again. She was right. We weren't getting out through there.

"OK then," he said. "I guess we'll just have to go the long way."

Quickly, but quietly, we made our way through the school. We had no idea if or when the wish might wear off, and we didn't want to be caught sneaking around if or when it did.

It was surreal, everything was perfectly silent. Peering through windows and doors, we saw snapshots of all the classrooms. Teachers were caught mid-conversation. Kids were passing notes, or sneaking glances at their phones.

In one classroom, we found a tall red-haired boy frozen in a state of panic. His paper aeroplane was locked on a collision course with the back of Mr Carson's head.

"Hey, wait a minute," I whispered to the other two.

They looked back at me with confused expressions.

Not wasting time on an explanation. I ran into Mr Carson's class and turned the aeroplane towards an open window. The boy would never know it was me, but that was my good deed of the day done.

Feeling proud of myself, I hurried back to my friends. Continuing along the corridor, we finally reached a side door that led out to the front gate. Holding my breath, I twisted the iron handle and pushed.

With a squeak and a groan, it swung open.

We were free.

With the outside world in sight, Absy broke into a run. Breathing a sigh of relief, I then did the same, closely followed by Kaya. In what was possibly the fastest one-hundred-metre sprint the school had ever seen, we soon found ourselves at the iron gates.

But there was a problem.

"They're locked," Kaya pointed out, catching her breath.

We all stared down at the thick chain and padlock holding them together.

"What do we do?" she asked.

"Climb over?" Absy suggested.

"It's too tall,"

Out of nowhere, I felt a shiver run through my body. Just like earlier, it felt like someone was watching us.

Something caught my eye in the field opposite the school. Beneath a large oak tree at the field's edge stood a dark and shadowy figure.

At first, I thought it might have been a farmer, frozen like the rest of the world, but then it moved. Slowly it raised its hand and snapped its fingers.

The chains fell away from the gate.

"What did you do?" Kaya asked, looking at me.

"Nothing," I replied. "It was—"

I looked back up, but the once again figure was gone.

Suddenly the world kicked back into motion. A chorus of sounds erupted from the silence, the wind started rustling in the trees, and birds started chirping back and forth. In the distance, I could hear a car engine racing through the countryside.

"It was what?" Kaya pressed.

"It doesn't matter," Absy interrupted. "We need to get out of here before someone sees us."

10

"What do we do now?" I asked.

"We lay low," Absy replied.

Kaya gave him a disapproving glare.

We'd found a quiet spot by a small shallow stream, hidden from the rest of the world by a thick hedgerow. We realised pretty quickly that there was nowhere else we could go. If we returned to school we'd be sent back to the office. If we got spotted in town, then our parents might find out and our lives would not be worth living.

"I spy with my little—" Absy started.

"No," Kaya said sharply.

Absy started kicking at the water in the stream.

"Well, we've got to do something to pass the time," he said.

"I know," Kaya agreed, "but not that."

"OK then," Absy thought for a moment, then smiled. "How about we make another wish?"

There was an awkward silence.

"I'm not sure we should," I said eventually.

"Why not?" He whined.

"Because we don't know what it does," Kaya said simply.

"It grants wishes." Absy looked at her confused.

"Yes, but how?" She paused. "What if every time you make a wish, something bad happens to someone else? Would you still use it then?"

"If that person is Verity Gowers, I reckon I could live with it," he grinned.

"Not funny," came Kaya's blunt reply.

"Come on, nothing bad has happened so far," he said.

"That you know of," she added.

"Fine, the two of you might be scared of it, but I'm not." He held his hand out towards me. "Give it here, I'll find out for myself."

I gripped the coin tightly in my pocket and shook my head.

"This is ridiculous." He started pacing back and forth. "Are you seriously telling me there is nothing you would wish for?"

"Of course there is," Kaya argued back, "but I don't think it's worth the risk. Not until we know more."

Absy turned his attention to me.

"And you, Tyler," he said. "Nothing you want to wish for?"

"No," I replied.

"Nothing at all?" he pressed.

"What do you want me to say?" I said.

"I want you to make a wish!"

"Be careful," I warned him, "because right now, I wish you'd be quiet."

He opened his mouth to argue back, but nothing came out. He tried again, but it was still just silence.

Kaya looked at me.

"What happened?" she asked nervously.

I pulled my hand out of my pocket and opened my fist. The small gold coin glinted back at me from the palm of my hand.

"I am so sorry," I said, realising what I'd done. "It was an accident!"

Absy pointed frantically at his mouth, as Kaya began to giggle.

"I'll undo it," I promised, wrapping my fingers around the coin.

"Do we have to?" Kaya's giggle was growing by the second as Absy flapped his arms more and more dramatically.

"I wish Absy had his voice back!"

"That was not funny," he scowled.

As a wave of relief washed over me, a smile crept across my face.

"It was kind of funny," I admitted.

Slowly his face cracked as he joined the laughter.

"Do another one," he said.

I hesitated for a moment, but then I gave into temptation. After all, nothing bad had happened yet.

"I guess I am kind of hungry." I gripped the coin tightly. "I wish we had pizza."

Nothing happened.

"Did it work?" Absy asked.

"I don't know," I replied, looking around.

"What's that?" Kaya pointed to a rock on the other side of the stream, on top of which was a large flat takeaway box.

Eagerly we all rushed over and lifted the lid. Inside was a hot and steamy pizza, topped with meat, peppers, onions, and extra cheese. It smelt amazing.

Without a second thought, we all dived in.

"Do you reckon you could wish for some garlic and herb dip?" Absy mumbled around a mouthful of pizza.

Whilst we sat and demolished our impromptu feast, we discussed what other wishes we could make. We covered everything from money to fame, and from super yachts to superpowers.

Time flew by and before we knew it hours had passed. Reaching into my pocket I pulled out my phone and lit up the screen.

Five messages from Dad.

I let out a groan.

"What is it?" Kaya asked.

"My dad has text me five times," I replied.

"Saying what?" There was a hint of panic in Absy's voice. "Do you think they know we ditched class?"

"He's reminding me to walk home with my sister after school." I slid my phone back into my pocket. "My family are the worst when it comes to stuff like this. Like, what is the big drama? I wish they'd just leave me alone."

"But that's good," Kaya said. "It means he thinks you're still there."

Absy's head popped up like a meerkat.

"Did you hear that?"

Me and Kaya stared at him in confusion.

"Hear what?" I asked.

He placed a finger over his lip and crawled towards the hedgerow. Slowly, he pulled back a couple of branches and peered through.

I could feel my heart thudding in my chest as he turned back to look at us.

"School's out," he announced with a grin.

11

Walking against the flood of people, the three of us headed for the school gates.

"We'll find Emily and we'll get out of there," I said. "If we're quick, then no one will even notice us."

"Remind me why we have to do this?" Absy whispered, glancing nervously over his shoulder.

"My parents are expecting me to come back with my sister. If I don't, I'm dead meat," I replied. "When we spot her, I'll go get her. I just need the two of you to keep an eye out for teachers."

"It's Mrs Allen we really need to watch out for," Kaya pointed out. "If she sees us coming back, we are one hundred percent busted."

As we got closer, we hid ourselves behind a group of boys from the year above. They were kicking a football against the wall whilst they stood chatting, providing perfect cover for us.

"Can you see her?" Kaya asked.

I craned my neck, trying to get a better look.

"Stop it." She pulled at my arm. "You're making it too obvious."

"OK, well you try and do better," I snapped back.

"Fine," she said. "Move over."

She pushed me to the side and slowly leaned out to look around the boys.

"Yeah, that's much more subtle," I whispered to Absy.

"I don't see her," Kaya said.

"Maybe she left already," Absy suggested.

"I can't risk it," I replied. "If I leave her waiting for me again, my parents will go mental."

"Just tell them you couldn't find her," he said. "Technically it's the truth."

"Technically isn't good enough. Come on, let's get closer." They took a step back. "OK, fine then, you wait here, and I'll take a look."

Doing my best ninja impression, I skulked through the crowd of green blazers. My eyes scanned the crowd for my sister's mop of curly brown hair. I'd almost made it to the gate, but she was still nowhere to be seen.

Above all the noise around me, I heard the call of a bird.

Caw-caw.

I turned on the spot, trying to find where it came from. Through the masses, I saw Absy standing with his hands cupped around his mouth. Next to him,

Kaya was pointing at something behind me, her eyes wide.

I followed her gaze and my heart sank.

There stood Mrs Allen, and she was staring right at me.

"Heads up!"

A stray football landed between us, distracting her for a split second. But that was all I needed.

I ran.

I ran as quickly as my legs would carry me, dodging and weaving through groups of people as I went. When I passed Kaya and Absy, I signalled for them to do the same.

We were halfway down the road when Absy called out to me.

"I think we're safe." He started slowing to a stop. "If I run any further, that pizza is going to come back up again."

He was bent over double as me and Kaya walked back to him.

"That was close," Kaya said. "Did she see you?"

"I think so," I nodded. "She was looking right at me."

Kaya let out a sigh.

"Was your sister there?"

I shook my head.

"It doesn't make sense," I said. "If Dad sent me five texts, you can guarantee he sent the same to her. There is no way she'd leave without me."

"Well, it looks like she did." Absy took a deep breath and stood up straight. "We should get back to town before your dad sends out a search party again."

He was right. At least if I wasn't too far behind Emily, I could say she left without me.

Without wasting another minute we headed straight for Lochview. Cutting across the fields and jumping a few fences, we managed to make good time to the café.

Standing at the door I hesitated for a moment.

"It's alright," Absy whispered. "If they try to tell you off, we'll back you up."

I turned to Kaya and she gave a supportive nod.

"OK, here we go."

I twisted the handle and pushed open the door, but all it revealed was an empty room.

There was no one there.

"Hello?" I called out. "Mum? Dad? Emily?"

Nothing.

Not so much as a sound.

"Maybe they're out back," Kaya said.

"Yeah, probably," I replied. "I'll go take a look."

As I headed through to the kitchen, my stomach started twisting and turning. Something was wrong, I'd felt it the instant I walked in the door. As I searched through the back rooms, I only confirmed what I already knew deep down.

There was no one here.

I returned to the others and shook my head.

"They probably had to run home for something," Absy said, trying his best to be reassuring. "I bet they'll pull up any minute. Don't worry though, we'll wait with you."

"They didn't go home," I replied bluntly.

"You don't know that—" he started.

"Actually, I do," I said, maybe a little too forcefully. "Their car is parked across the road."

12

Something really weird was happening, and there was only one person I could call when that was the case.

"Master Tyler, Miss Kaya." Archie removed his hat and greeted us with a nod, before turning to Absy. "I don't believe have met."

"This is Absy," I said. "Absy, this is Archie Macleod."

"A pleasure." Archie held out his hand, and Absy awkwardly shook it. "Now, I trust this isn't a social visit. What do you need?"

"Have you seen my parents today?" I asked.

"Not since this morning," he replied. "Is everything alright?"

I glanced at Absy and Kaya before turning back to Archie.

"OK, different question," I said. "What do you know about Fae?"

"Why?" Archie's eyebrows raised quizzically.

"No reason."

"Tyler Buckland, I may be many things, but an idiot is not one of them." He took off his jacket and placed it on a chair. "I assume you have called me here because you find yourself in some form of trouble. So, I am going to go and make us some tea, and the three of you are going to get your story straight. When I return, we will all sit down together, and you can start from the beginning."

Archie had barely stepped into the back room before Absy started to voice his objections.

"I don't get it," he said. "Who even is he?"

"He lives next door to me," I explained, "in the manor."

"Woah, hang on." I could see the realisation dawn on Absy's face. "Is that Mad Man Macleod?"

"He prefers Archie," I replied disapprovingly.

"OK, but I don't see how he can help," He protested. "If this coin really is Fae, then we should be talking to Mr McPhee."

"If I remember rightly, the last time we saw Mr McPhee he was kicking us out of his shop because someone was opening things he shouldn't have been," Kaya butted in. "Besides, Mr McPhee is creepy."

Tempers were beginning to flare, and I knew that wasn't going to help anyone. Absy opened his mouth to argue back, but I got there first.

"Archie knows about this kind of stuff," I explained calmly. "It's also not the first time we've had to deal with something like this."

I could feel Kaya's eyes glaring at me, but if we were going to fix this, then Absy had a right to know the truth.

"What do you mean?" he asked.

"What I am about to tell you can go no further," I told him. "You have to promise me."

He nodded nervously.

"You know Jackson Weir?"

"Yes," he said quietly.

"We know what happened to him." The words caught in my throat. "He was taken by the Lady of the Loch."

"But she's just a—" he began.

"A story?" Kaya said. "Turns out, she was pretty real."

"Was real?" Absy questioned. "What happened to her?"

"Young Master Tyler stopped her." Archie reappeared in the doorway with a tray of mugs. "Now, if we are all on the same page, perhaps you could be so kind as to tell me why you called."

We told him everything, from visiting The Beyond to making Verity eat worms. Though Absy did make a point of clarifying it was an accident. A happy one, but an accident nonetheless. He listened intently to every detail of our escape from the Headteacher's office, and of our lunch down by the stream.

"There's something else," I said as our story came to an end, "I think someone has been watching us."

Archie looked over the rim of his red tartan glasses.

"And what makes you think that?" he asked.

"It happened after Verity ate the worms, and when time was frozen." I was trying to explain, but it was hard. "There was this shadow. I couldn't see who it was, but it was definitely a person."

"OK." Archie pondered everything we had told him. "You're sure there is nowhere else your parents might have gone?"

I shook my head.

"The car is outside, and the café was unlocked, I've tried calling but neither of them are answering." I could feel the panic building inside me.

"Your sister?"

"The same."

He thought for a moment.

"May I see the coin?" He held his hand out towards me.

I reached into my pocket and pulled it out, but before I placed it in his palm I stopped.

My heart started racing.

"What's wrong?" Archie asked tentatively.

I tried to speak but the words wouldn't come out.

What I held between my fingers was not the coin Absy had taken from The Beyond. Though its markings were the same, its once shiny gold surface was now dull and brown. Flecks of rust crumbled onto my fingertips.

Kaya turned to me, her eyes wide with fear, and whispered five haunting words.

"The price has been paid."

13

"What do you mean?" I asked. "What price?"

Everyone was staring at Kaya. She started to squirm uncomfortably.

"It crossed my mind earlier," she explained. "I didn't want to say anything because I hoped I was wrong."

"Kaya, just spit it out." I could feel the frustration building inside of me.

"Well, we know the coin grants wishes," she continued, "but what if there is something darker to it? What if it gives you want, but then it takes something in return?"

"So I make a wish and it takes my family?" I cried in disbelief. "How is that fair?"

"No one ever said it was fair." She countered.

Without warning Absy bolted out of his chair.

"Where are you going?" I asked, grabbing his arm. "It's your fault we're in this mess, and now you're going to leave?"

"I need to make a call," he replied.

"Right now?" I couldn't believe he was being so selfish. "You have to make a call right this minute?"

"Yes, I do," he said breaking free from my grip. "You weren't the only one who made a wish."

A pang of guilt hit me like a punch in the gut. I'd been so wrapped up in what was happening to me that I didn't even think about Absy. We all watched silently as he tried to call his parents.

Once, twice, three times.

No answer.

"They're not picking up," he said, his voice trembling.

"What do we do?" I asked, looking to Archie.

"Well, I guess—"

"I don't care what you guys do," Absy interrupted. "I'm going to Mr McPhee."

He turned to leave.

"Absy, wait." I stopped him as he reached for the door. "You're right, we need to go back to The Beyond, but none of us are going alone. If we're going to fix this, we'll fix it together."

He nodded, tears forming in his eyes.

"Thank you."

"Whilst you do that, I feel it might be wise for me to consult the library at the manor," Archie suggested. "Perhaps there is an entry in the archives that might be of service."

He rose to his feet and folded his jacket over his arm.

"I wish you all the best of luck, and as always, if I am required, you need only to call."

"Thank you, Archie," I said with a nod.

Before leaving, he reached into his pocket and pulled out a large bundle of keys. They jingled in his hand as he rifled through, before stopping on a small silver one. He removed it from the ring and placed it in my hand. I looked back at him, confused.

"Your parents left me a spare for the café," he explained. "It is probably best you lock up when you leave."

Bidding goodbye to the others, he climbed into his car and headed back towards the Manor.

"We should go," Absy said. "Mr McPhee will be closing up soon."

I headed towards the door, but Kaya didn't budge. She just sat in her chair, staring off into space.

"Kaya, are you OK?" I asked.

"Yeah, sorry." She gave herself a shake. "I was just thinking about something."

"Anything important?" Absy chimed in from the doorway.

"No, honestly, it was nothing." She smiled and got to her feet. "Let's do this."

Locking the door behind us, we made our way down the high street. A cold chill swept over me as the stone entrance to the alleyway came into sight.

The cobblestone passage seemed somehow darker than before. In the cold shadows of the surrounding buildings it was like the sun had vanished altogether.

We stopped at the top of the stairs. The old wooden sign creaked softly in the wind. Below, the door to the shop lay open, inviting us inside.

"Who's going first?" I asked, hoping someone else would volunteer.

"I'll go," Absy said, and a wave of relief washed over me.

Slowly, he descended the stone steps into the darkness below. I took a deep breath, I fought every urge in my body that told me to turn and walk away, and I followed him into The Beyond.

As my eyes adjusted to the lack of light, my heart dropped like a stone.

The shop was deserted.

Though the air was still thick and heavy, the smell of scented smoke was gone. The crooked and uneven shelves that once housed otherworldly souvenirs lay barren. The horror-filled glass jars stood cracked and empty.

"Mr McPhee?" Absy called out, but no one replied.

Cautiously, we walked deeper into the shop.

"It looks like he left," Kaya said, running her finger through the dust on the shelves.

"Why though?" I pondered. "You don't just randomly pack up everything and leave. Something must have happened."

"Something did." Came a voice from behind us.

There was the small chime of a bell as the front door slammed shut. We spun on the spot to see Mr McPhee standing hunched between us and the only exit.

"What is it you want?" he asked in his cracked old voice. "And be quick about it, I have places to be."

"We need your help," Absy said, stepping forwards. He paused, considering his words. "We found this coin, and we think it might be Fae."

"Oh?" McPhee looked up with intrigue in his eyes. "And what makes you think that?"

Something began to stir in the very pit of my stomach.

"It grants wishes," Absy answered, "but it's taken our parents."

In the dim light of the shop, I could have sworn I saw a hint of a smile cross McPhee's lips.

"May I take a look?" He reached out his hand as he crept towards us with long unbroken strides.

Something was very wrong.

"Absy, get back" I whispered.

"Why?" Absy replied.

"Because that is not Mr McPhee."

Buzz!

It was the same noise I'd heard before the storm. It started small at first but quickly grew louder and louder as Mr McPhee transformed before us.

A glint of purple light flashed across the old man's

eyes. With each step he seemed to get taller, as he straightened up to his full height. His thin white hair was suddenly thick and dark, tied back neatly in a ponytail. His wrinkled skin was now smooth and grey, his face slender and sharp with an angular jaw and pointed chin.

Dressed in a deep purple three-piece suit, he tipped his top hat in our direction.

"Tell me, what is that gave me away?" He smiled, revealing a row of razor-sharp teeth.

We all stood staring in shocked silence.

"Come now, don't be like that," he said. "I really would like to know."

"Your walk," I stuttered, "Mr McPhee walks with a limp."

"The walk," he repeated, his voice raspy and quiet. "Such a small detail, yet still so very important."

"Who are you?" Absy asked nervously.

The creature's smile grew even wider.

"I am Cináed, and I believe you have something of mine."

14

Whilst me and Absy fumbled our words, trying desperately to find something to say, Kaya stepped in. Somehow despite everything we had just witnessed, she had kept her cool, unlike the two of us.

"If we have something you want," she said calmly, "then I would like to suggest a deal."

The creature's head turned excitedly.

"Would you now?" He grinned. "What, might I ask, are your terms?"

"The coin took Absy and Tyler's families as payment," she replied. "We want them back. You give us what we want, and we'll give you what you want."

"I like her," Cináed chuckled. "She's got some real fight in her blood. I am afraid, however, that on this occasion I will be declining your offer."

"What?" All of Kaya's confidence fell away in an instant. "But you can't. You're a Bòcan, you'd never refuse a deal."

"I would if the terms are not proper." The smile on his face was growing by the second. "You may think yourself clever, young lady, but your terms are impossible. Therefore, I say once again, no deal."

He licked his lips with glee.

I felt like I was going to be sick.

"Kaya, what is a Bòcan?" Absy whispered. He was clearly just as lost as I was.

"He's trouble," she replied. "A Bòcan is a Fae that has been corrupted by chaos and mischief. He is always willing to help, but only for a price."

"Good work deserves a good reward," the creature said smugly. "Speaking of which, perhaps we could get back to the matter at hand."

"What is wrong with our terms?" I asked, finally finding my voice. "Why are they impossible?"

"Simple," he answered, "There has been no payment made, therefore no payment can be returned. Even if I wanted to."

"What about our families?" Absy argued. "The coin took them."

"No, it did not!" A sudden wave of anger washed over his face, stopping Absy in his tracks. "Listen closely, boy, for no untruth shall ever pass these lips. Your family are safe and well, neither myself nor any objects associated with my personage have had any contact with them whatsoever."

Absy turned to Kaya.

"It's true," she said, "he can't lie."

70

"But, I called them," Absy protested.

"And perhaps they had better things to do than answer," Cináed replied coldly. "In future, I'd advise you to avoid jumping to conclusions when you are not in possession of all the facts."

"And my parents?" I asked.

"They were dealt with, as per your request."

"My request?" I felt a wave of panic slowly wash over me. "I never asked for this."

"No, you *wished* for it." He started to walk slowly towards me. "You wished for your family to leave you alone, and what better way to achieve that than by having them vanish altogether."

"OK, then I'll wish for them back."

"And how do you propose to do that?" His eyes locked unblinking on to mine. "Erasing your family takes a lot of power. I'd imagine your wishes are all used up. In fact, I'd wager that shiny golden coin is looking rather dull right now."

I ran my fingers over its rough and rusty surface in my pocket. There was a sinking feeling in my chest.

"Now I could bring them back, I could make you a deal, but first there is the matter of an outstanding payment." He stopped, his face a matter of inches from mine. Then slowly he turned to Absy.

"What payment?" Absy asked, his voice trembling.

"You took something that didn't belong to you, something that comes with a price." Cináed stood up to his full height. "I expect you to pay it."

"I don't have any money," Absy whimpered.

"I don't want your money." The creature's eyes lit up. "I want your soul."

Absy started to back away.

"What, like when I die?" he asked.

The Bòcan laughed.

"No, I like mine a little fresher than that."

Absy was cornered, his back pressed against the wall. The Bòcan reached its long spindly fingers towards him, its nails black and broken.

"Please don't," he begged, but it was no use.

The creature's pointed teeth were on full display as he savoured every moment.

"Absy, run!" Kaya screamed.

In one swift movement, she opened the locket on her necklace, releasing a fine grey powder into her palm. Pushing herself in front of Absy, she blew it into Cináed's face.

There was a horrifying sizzle as it made contact with his cold grey flesh.

"The door!" She yelled, dragging me and Absy towards the exit.

Cináed clutched his face, screaming in agony.

"This isn't over!" He cried. "I will have what is mine!"

15

Dark clouds rolled in overheard as we reached the main road. A torrent of rain lashed down on the pavement whilst lightning ripped through the sky above.

Taking the lead, I bolted up the high street, heading for the edge of town.

"Where are we going?" Absy shouted, following close behind with Kaya.

"Somewhere safe," I replied. "Just trust me."

My lungs were on fire, and my heart was beating so fast it felt like it was about to burst, but I couldn't stop. The thought of Cináed lurking in the shadows behind us spurred me on. The thought of his shark-like grin sent goosebumps up the back of my neck.

I knew we couldn't outrun him forever, but we could at least try to outrun him for now.

We raced past the last few houses on the edge of Lochview, cutting through a hedge into the fields beyond. In the distance I could see the deep wood that stood between the town and home.

Slam!

Absy crashed hard into the mud.

"Are you OK?" Kaya exclaimed, rushing over to him.

"I must have caught my leg on a root or something," he grimaced, rolling up his trouser leg.

"We need to keep moving," I said urgently. "Come on, it's not much further."

"Tyler, stop." Kaya put her hand on my shoulder. "I think we're safe."

"Do you?" I bit back. "Do you think we're safe? Because I just watched some evil fairy try to steal Absy's soul. The same evil fairy, in fact, who has taken my family. All thanks to a wish that I didn't even realise I'd made."

"I'm sorry," she said quietly. "I didn't mean—"

"What didn't you mean?" I asked, cutting her off. "Or is it a secret? Because there definitely seems to be a lot you're not telling us lately."

She looked down at her feet.

I shouldn't have been angry with her, after all, she had just single-handedly saved our lives. Yet I couldn't stop myself. My mind was going a mile a minute, trying to make sense of everything that had happened.

"How did you know what that thing was?" I asked her.

"My gran," she replied. "She used to know everything there was to know about Fair Folk, all the

74

legends and the stories. When I'd visit her on a Sunday, she'd show me all her books and pictures, it was all we'd ever talk about."

Kaya held her necklace between her fingers.

"She gave me this. She told me it would protect me if I was to ever find myself on the wrong side of a Fae." She smiled gently. "I used to think it was silly, but I guess she was right."

"Hang on," Absy stepped in. "If your gran knows so much about Fae, then why don't we go speak to her?"

"We can't." Kaya shook her head. "She died last year."

"I'm sorry," I said, and I meant it with all my heart. I felt the anger wash away, replaced by a wave of guilt. It wasn't her fault we were in this mess. She had only ever tried to help.

"What do we do now?" Absy asked, breaking the silence.

"We need to get back to the Manor," I told him. "Hopefully Archie has found something we can use."

"And if he hasn't?"

"We know what we're up against now. Believe me, we'll find something." I flashed him a reassuring smile, but inside I was terrified.

Cináed was powerful, there was no denying it. Though no one would say it out loud, I think we all knew there would be no easy way to stop him.

But that didn't mean we wouldn't try.

We trudged on through the muddy fields. Then we made our way as quickly as we could through the dense woods. All the while keeping one eye open for anyone or anything that might be lurking in the shadows.

Finally, the Manor came into view. By the time we reached its heavy wooden doors, my legs were ready to give way beneath me. I reached for the large iron knocker, but Archie appeared before I even had the chance to touch it.

"Get yourselves inside," he said, hurrying us towards the drawing room. "Look at the three of you, you're drenched. Take a seat by the fire and get warmed up."

The heat of the fire hit me from the moment I stepped into the room. We took a seat on the sofa, each of us shivering from the cold.

"I'll fetch some towels," Archie said. "Perhaps a cup of tea as well."

"Thank you." I tried to smile, but my cheeks hadn't quite defrosted yet.

"You're welcome." He nodded. "Then, once you are all dry, I have something that you may wish to see."

16

Archie dropped a large dusty tome on the table in front of us. Its dark leather cover was worn and cracked with age. I could only just make out the title, written in faded gold lettering.

"The Sith of Lochview," I read.

"It's pronounced *shee*" Kaya corrected. "It's the Gaelic word for Fair Folk."

"Very good, Miss Kaya." Archie smiled approvingly. "This is an encyclopaedia of local Fae. It was compiled by Eustace Dowell way back in the early thirteenth Century. In fact, it even predates this manor by over one hundred years. Now, I had started to bookmark some pages that I thought might be of interest. Perhaps there might be some mention of this shadowy figure you saw, Tyler."

"His name is Cináed," I said, much to Archie's surprise.

"Cináed?" he repeated. "How do you know that?"

"He told us," I replied.

"And he's a Bòcan," Kaya added. "It's a type of Fae."

Archie looked between the three of us, his eyes wide. He seemed a little shocked by how much we had discovered since we'd all sat together in the cafe.

"What exactly happened in that shop?" he asked nervously.

"Well, we found Mr McPhee," I explained. "Only it wasn't him, it was the Bòcan. He told us he wants payment for the stolen coin, but we refused because the payment he wants is Absy's soul. So Kaya blinded him and we ran."

His mouth fell open. I could almost see the cogs turning in his head.

"Hang on a minute." Archie held up his hands. "What about your parents? I thought they were the payment."

"Actually, that is something else," I said awkwardly. "It turns out that I might have accidentally wished my family away. It would also appear that the only way to get them back would involve making a deal with the Bòcan."

"My family is OK though," Absy jumped in. "They just weren't answering the phone."

"Well at least there is one positive," Archie said with a sigh. "So, what do we do now?"

"We don't know," I said simply. "I'm not sure there is anything we can do."

Everyone fell silent. The only sound was the fire

crackling softly. Its flames dancing gently in the shadows of the hearth.

The more I thought about it, the more impossible it seemed. Cináed was too powerful, he could be anyone and he could do anything. We were just three school kids and a tour guide, hardly the most formidable team.

"We need to change how we are looking at this." Kaya rose purposefully from her chair and started pacing back and forth in front of the fireplace. "At the moment, Cináed is holding all the cards, but what if we changed that? What if we had an ace up our sleeve?"

We all stared at her blankly.

"He's a Bòcan," she said, as if we would all suddenly understand where she was going with this. "Bòcan's make deals. It's in their blood, they can't resist it. We just need to find something he wants."

"I am not giving him my soul," Absy objected.

"Then we find something else," she shot back. "There has to be something he wants, something we can use to bargain with."

"His freedom." It was like a lightbulb had switched on in Archie's head. Opening the book, he started turning frantically through the pages. "Here!"

We all leant in.

Archie had stopped on a page filled with wild scribblings and rough diagrams. The ink had blotted and ran, and the words barely looked like English.

"What is it?" I asked.

"These are traps," Archie replied. "The ones Eustace describes are fairly small, but if we could increase the size—"

"Then maybe we could trap a Bòcan," Kaya finished.

"Precisely," he nodded, "and once our Fae friend is captured, he might be a little more open to negotiation."

We all watched excitedly as Archie ran his fingers along the page, deciphering the scrawling text.

"We can certainly get our hands on everything it says we require, but then we hit a problem."

My heart sank.

"What's the problem?" I was looking at the book, but still couldn't make out a word of what was written.

"It says here that the trap must be set at a gate," he explained.

"There's a gate at the end of the driveway," Absy pointed out.

"Not that kind of gate." Archie shook his head. "It must be set at a gateway between our world and theirs. I don't know about the three of you, but I have never seen one marked on a map before."

"So, it's another dead end?" I sat back with a sigh.

"Maybe not," Kaya said quietly. She stood watching the fire, her eyes locked on the dancing flames.

"You know where to find a gate?" I asked.

"Not quite," she answered, "but I know how to contact someone who might."

She then turned to face us, before making one of the strangest requests I've ever heard.

"I'm going to need some milk and a stone bowl."

17

The milk was easy to find, the stone bowl less so. Eventually, we found a stone mortar tucked away in the back of a cupboard in the kitchen.

"It will have to do," Kaya said taking it back through to the drawing room.

We all watched as she placed the bowl on the windowsill, before filling it with milk and opening the windows. The fire flickered as a cold breeze swept through the room.

"What now?" I asked.

"We wait I guess," she replied, taking a seat. "I can't say I've ever tried to summon a Fae before."

It was a fair point. None of us really knew what was going on, but as things stood, this was the only idea we had. So all we could do was simply sit and hope.

Gradually the minutes turned into hours, yet still there was nothing. Even as the sun began to set in the distance, we were still sat waiting for something to happen.

But there was nothing.

There was no one flying in through the window, no one bursting forth from the fire, there wasn't even anything as boring as a knock at the door.

"We should get the two of you home," Archie said to Kaya and Absy. "It's getting late. Your parents will be wondering where you are."

"But the Bòcan—" Absy protested.

"Has had all afternoon to make an appearance," Archie replied calmly. "There is nothing more we can do tonight."

"I can ask my mum to pick us up," Kaya offered. "We don't want a Fae to show up when we're not here."

"That would be very helpful," he smiled. "Thank you."

All the while I sat quietly.

I didn't have a family to go back to, at least not anymore.

"Tyler," Archie said softly. "Perhaps you would like to spend the night here. There is more than enough room."

"Thanks," I replied with a grateful smile.

A wave of relief washed over me, the thought of spending a night alone in that empty house sent a shiver down my spine.

When Kaya's mum arrived to collect her and Absy, Archie walked me down to my house. Although we didn't want to leave the manor, I needed to pick up a few things and didn't want to go alone.

Standing at the end of our garden path, I could feel the nerves starting to flutter in my stomach. I walked along it every day without a care in the world, but today it felt different.

The silence was the first thing to hit me as I opened the front door. At the very least I'd normally hear the sound of a TV blaring or a kettle boiling, but there was nothing.

It was unnaturally quiet.

I quickly made my way to my bedroom, not even bothering to turn on the lights along the way. Grabbing some clothes and my toothbrush, I threw everything I needed in a bag and ran back downstairs. I didn't want to be there one second longer than I had to.

Archie was waiting in the kitchen.

"Got everything?" he asked.

"Yeah, I think so," I replied, heading straight for the door.

As I reached for the handle, he stopped me.

"We will get them back," he said, placing his hand on my shoulder.

"I know." I forced a smile and stepped outside.

In reality, I had no idea if I'd see my family again, but I couldn't give up hope. We would find a way, we had to.

The rest of the evening was spent keeping watch in the drawing room. Once I found my spot on the sofa, I didn't move an inch. Archie vanished for a while to make dinner, and even when he returned, I was still sitting in the exact same place.

Whilst we ate, I kept one eye trained on the open window. Despite the darkness outside, there was still enough light from the moon to make out rough shapes. Not that there was anything to see, just a few trees blowing gently in the breeze.

"Maybe we should call it a night," Archie suggested, rubbing his eyes. "It's getting late."

"Just a little while longer," I begged.

"You are of no use to anyone exhausted," he replied. "It's time for bed."

I wanted to argue, but I didn't have the strength. Plus, deep down, I knew he was right.

Despite my best efforts to fight the tiredness that was slowly creeping in, my eyelids were getting heavier by the minute. With a yawn and a stretch, I got to my feet.

"We'll try all this again in the morning," he said, closing the windows.

"No wait, leave them open." I looked at him pleadingly. "Just in case."

He hesitated a moment, then gave a nod.

"Of course." He smiled warmly, then headed for the door. "Come on then, I'll show you to your room."

He led me to a room upstairs at the very furthest end of the manor. Looking back down the hallway I could barely see the staircase down to the front door.

"I'm afraid I couldn't put you any closer," he apologised. "The other rooms are all laid out for tours."

It seemed a lifetime ago that I'd first explored Lochview Manor on one of Archie's infamous ghost tours. Who knows, maybe one day there will be a tour guide telling my story. The tale of the boy who accidentally wished away his parents.

I thanked Archie for his help and said goodnight.

When I flicked the light switch, my jaw nearly hit the floor.

The room was huge.

A large four-poster bed, draped in green, took up most of the space. What remained was filled with dark wood cabinets and chests of drawers, and a massive desk with an equally giant mirror.

It felt like I was sleeping in a medieval castle.

Though when I thought about how old this room must be, I practically was sleeping in a medieval castle.

I got myself ready for bed, then slid under the heavy silk covers. At first, it felt weird, lying there in this strange old bed, but it wasn't long before sleep took hold.

Then it happened.

Then something went bump in the night.

18

At first, I thought I'd dreamt it.

I climbed out of bed and turned on the light. Slowly, I made my way to the door, the wooden floor creaking gently beneath my feet. I stepped out into the hallway, using the torch on my phone to fight against the darkness.

The light washed over the portrait of a stony-faced man. His bushy sideburns and thick moustache gave him a pompous air of nobility. At first glance he looked kind of funny, but the longer I stared the more it felt like its eyes were watching me.

It's just a picture.

Ahead I heard a soft groan, like the sound of a door opening.

"Hello?" I called out along the corridor. "Archie, is that you?"

Nothing.

Just silence.

Cautiously I crept forward. My eyes darted from door to door, watching like a hawk for even the slightest sign of movement.

"Archie, are you there?" I tried again.

I didn't like this. It was way too quiet. Inside, my stomach was twisting into knots.

In the dark the Manor took on a whole new life. All the shadows felt deeper, the creaks and groans felt louder, and the long hallways felt never-ending.

I passed a picture of a large woman with tight curly hair and got a sudden sense of de ja vu. Stopping, I looked closer at the portrait. I'd walked past it already, I was sure of it. I turned to look back, but all I could see was the same oak panelling stretching off into nothingness.

Slam!

I froze.

It came from downstairs.

Looking ahead, I could now see the bannister at the top of the staircase in the front hall. My gut twisted tighter. I was certain it hadn't been there a second ago.

I thought about calling for Archie again, but I knew there was no use. Whatever was going on, I was going to have to face it myself.

Reaching the top of the stairs I looked down into the foyer. There was a faint glow of light coming from the corridor below.

With a deep breath, I made my way down.

The door to the drawing room lay slightly ajar, just enough for a warm orange light to flicker out into the hallway. I placed my hand gently against its smooth wood, peering inside.

A dark shape stood by the window. I strained my eyes to see more, but in the dim light I couldn't make out who, or what, it was.

Creak!

I leaned too hard against the door and it edged open. My heart stopped as the shadowy figure turned quickly on the spot.

"Come in, Tyler. It's only me."

I pushed the door further and saw Archie's face looking back at me.

"Be careful where you put your feet," he said, scanning the room with a quizzical expression. "They appear to have made quite the mess?"

"Who?" I asked.

"I have no idea."

The drawing room, that only hours before had been completely pristine, was now covered in small patches of black soot. They covered the floor, the sofa, some had even made it onto the wall.

"Are they—" I started, pointing down at one of the marks.

"Footprints?" Archie finished. "Yes, I believe they are."

"But they're tiny." I crouched down to inspect one closer. There was the clear shape of a foot accompanied by five tiny dots, but it couldn't have been much longer than two or three inches.

"They would have to be," he replied. "If they were any bigger they wouldn't have fit down the chimney."

"But, the fire—"

"My thoughts exactly." He reached down and picked up the mortar that lay toppled over on the floor, surrounded by a small puddle of milk. "It is all a little peculiar."

"Whatever it was, it can't have been alone," I pointed out, following the footprints as they weaved and crossed each other. "There must have been at least four, maybe five of them."

The prints all came to a stop in a mound of ash that covered the stone hearth of the fireplace.

"Archie, I think you should come look at this," I said.

"What is it?" He wandered over, stopping beside me. "Oh, I see."

Carved into the ash, by what must have been really tiny fingers, were three words.

Seelie Point. Noon.

19

When morning came, I found Archie in the kitchen making breakfast. I hovered quietly at the door, waiting for him to notice me.

We hadn't actually discussed whether or not I would still be going to school. After everything that happened, I felt like I deserved a day off. I'd even left my uniform at home in case it would help to sway any discussion in my favour.

Unfortunately, it didn't.

"Your parents would want you to go to school," Archie said, much to my dismay.

"My parents aren't here," I argued back.

"Which is why I have to act in their stead." He placed a plate of toast in front of me. "Now, have some breakfast, and then we'll go and get your uniform."

I dropped myself into a seat at the table. I made sure to keep eye contact with Archie as I ate, just to ensure he could see I was sulking.

It wasn't fair. With everything going on, how could he possibly think that sending me to school was the right thing to do?

"What about Seelie Point?" I asked, trying a different approach.

"I will go," he said, "and then I will inform you of what transpires when I pick you up from school."

"What if it's a trap?" I pressed. "What if it was Cináed that left that message? What if you go up there alone and he takes you too?"

"Then we will have had a lucky escape," he said, adjusting his glasses. "For if I go alone, then you, Kaya and Absy will still be free to find another way to stop him."

I crossed my arms.

He was infuriating. No matter what I said, he had an answer.

"If you are quite finished, we should get moving." He took my empty plate and placed it in the sink.

Knock, knock, knock!

We both looked at each other. Judging by the look on Archie's face, he wasn't expecting visitors.

"Wait here," he said, before striding out into the foyer.

I waited for a second, then decided to follow him instead. I hung back, watching around the corner, out of sight in the shadows

Reaching for the handle, he had barely turned it an inch before the door burst open.

"Good morning, Mr Macleod." Absy bounded in, closely followed by Kaya who was a little more restrained. "Any updates from last night?"

I stepped out of the shadows with an excited smile on my face.

"Actually, there is," I said.

It was good to see the two of them, to know they were still safe.

"Hang on a minute." Archie raised his voice, so he could be heard over our chatter. "Should the two of you not be getting ready for school?"

"We can't, I'm afraid," Absy said, pretending to cough in his hand. "We're sick."

"But won't they call your parents if you're not there?" I asked.

"Let's just say I'm very good at sounding like my dad on the phone." He grinned proudly.

Archie glared at him disapprovingly.

"I don't think it's right either, Archie," Kaya said sympathetically. "But maybe some things are more important than school."

I looked at him pleadingly, surely he couldn't make me go if Kaya and Absy weren't.

"One day off," he said sternly. "I'll make the call, you take them through to the drawing room."

"What's in the drawing room?" Kaya asked.

"I'll show you."

The moment I opened the door, their eyes widened. Archie and I had left the room exactly how we'd found it the night before. Except for the milk, he was worried that might start to smell.

"She was right!" Kaya exclaimed, eagerly analysing each of the tiny footprints. "Gran was right. Everyone always said she was mad, but she was right."

"There's more," I said, pointing them in the direction of the fireplace.

They looked at me in disbelief.

"What are we waiting for?" Absy smiled. "Let's go."

"Hang on," I said, calming him down. "Let's not rush into anything. For all we know, Cináed has planned all this. Maybe the Fae are all on his side."

"OK, then we protect ourselves," Absy shrugged. "Kaya, any chance your gran left you more weapons we can use?"

"We can't," she replied, shaking her head. "If we want their help, then we have to trust them. If we walk in there ready for a fight, they will turn on us in an instant. You both saw The Beyond, all those traps and cages. Let's face it, humans haven't always been the kindest when it comes to Fae."

It didn't sit well with me, but she had a point. We needed them, not the other way around. So, we had to show them that we came in peace, even if that meant leaving ourselves vulnerable.

Absy went to argue but was interrupted by Archie appearing at the door with an empty rucksack.

"Go into the kitchen and grab some supplies," he said, holding it out to us. "We should get moving if we are going to make it there by noon."

"Supplies?" I questioned, but the other two just nodded and took the bag. "How far away is Seelie Point?"

"Far enough," Archie replied. "I hope you're not afraid of heights."

20

We had been walking uphill for what felt like an eternity.

Since leaving the manor, I'd learned that Seelie Point stood at the very top of one of the larger hills that surrounded Loch Dowell. Archie spent most of the journey there making it very clear that they were in fact hills. Apparently, they weren't quite tall enough to be mountains. Though based on the burning in my legs they might as well have been.

"It could be worse," Kaya said, clearly noticing my pain. "We could be climbing that."

She pointed off into the distance, towards a snow-covered peak high above the clouds.

Surely that had to be a mountain.

I dared not ask Archie, just in case we found ourselves receiving another surprise geography lesson. He still wasn't overly happy that we were missing school, so had taken it upon himself to ensure that we still learned something today.

Not that any of us were really listening anyway.

Kaya had explained that Seelie Point was a circle of stones looking out over Loch Dowell. No one knows for sure how the stones came to be there, but naturally there are plenty of stories.

Her Gran told her it was the meeting point of the Seelie Court. They were a group of Fae who believed in working with humanity, unlike the Unseelie Court who stood against us.

It was still so surreal to think this whole other world existed.

Had you told me a few days before that I would be climbing a hill in search of a group of Fairies, I'd have laughed in your face. Yet, here I was, doing just that.

Looking back over my shoulder I could see Lochview off towards the horizon. I wondered how many people walked those streets each day, thinking it was just a boring little town. If only they knew what really lay under the surface, the unbelievable things I'd seen.

As the crest of the hill came into sight, the nerves started to kick in.

I had no idea what to expect when we reached the top. None of us did. We kept glancing at each other out of the corner of our eyes, waiting for someone to speak.

But none of us knew what to say.

All we could do was hope that there was someone up there waiting to help us.

Or something.

The sun was high above us in the sky as we reached the summit.

In the grass before us there stood a circle of ten small stones. Each of which was partially buried in the ground, just as Kaya had described.

But that was it.

There was no one waiting.

There was no one there at all.

"What time is it?" Absy asked, looking around in confusion.

"One minute to," Kaya replied.

From where we stood we could see for miles in every direction. We were alone. I was sure of it.

"Well, this was a waste of time," Absy huffed, sitting on one of the stones. "This is him. It's that Fae messing with us, and we all fell for it."

Absy continued to moan, but I stopped listening.

Something else had drawn my attention.

Buzz!

It was quiet, but it was there. The same soft buzzing I'd heard in the shop, the same I'd heard the night of the storm. I looked around in panic.

"Can you hear that?" I asked.

Absy stopped midsentence.

"Hear what?" He asked, looking at me with concern in his eyes.

"There's a buzzing," I replied. "I've heard it before. I heard it when—"

I didn't get a chance to finish the sentence.

In an instant the world around us dissolved into darkness. The bright summer sky was gone, replaced by an empty black void.

It took a moment for my eyes to adjust, but when they did, I couldn't even begin to understand what I was seeing.

Although we were still standing in the stone circle from Seelie Point, we were no longer standing at the top of a hill. I wasn't even sure we were still on earth.

The circle had transported us to the heart of a deep dark wood, but the trees were unlike anything I'd seen before. Their branches gave off a pale white glow, it was dull, but it was also the only light we had.

"Where are we?" Absy asked, the panic clear in his voice.

"I don't know," Kaya replied. "Gran never mentioned anything like this."

As I looked around, my heart sank. It was just trees and darkness as far as the eye could see, stretching on and on into eternity.

"It was a trap," I said. "The message, the circle, everything. He planned it all, he's won."

"We don't know that," Archie argued. His words were optimistic, but I don't think even he really believed them.

"Yes, we do." I sat, defeated, on one of the stones. I could see the same disappointment on each of their faces.

Snap!

I jumped to my feet. The noise came from somewhere in the trees behind me.

"What was that?" Absy's voice was really trembling now.

Snap!

It was closer this time, like something was walking towards us, breaking twigs beneath its feet.

I stepped back towards the others. There was a soft rustling between the branches of the trees.

It started small, but slowly it began to spread until it surrounded us on all sides.

"Everyone stay close," I whispered to the others. "Whatever happens, just be ready to run."

"We're in a weird forest and we're surrounded," Kaya pointed out. "Where exactly are we meant to run to?"

She was right. There was nowhere to run to. There was no escape at all.

As the sound grew louder, I could feel my legs starting to shake beneath me.

Snap!

My heart thudded in my chest.

Just beyond the first line of trees, I saw something move in the shadows. My blood ran cold. There, staring back at me, were a pair of sinister purple eyes.

All of a sudden, the rustling stopped.

21

"Who's there?" I shouted, trying hard to hide my terror. "Show yourself."

There was a moment of silence, then something moved slowly towards us.

Out of the inky blackness stepped a small hairy man. He was thin and wiry, with long pointed ears and an almost triangular chin. His clothes were rough and dirty, hanging loosely over his slender frame.

"Let's make this quick," he said in a gruff voice. "We haven't much time."

"Who are you?" I asked, a little startled by his rough demeanour.

"*We*," he stressed, "are the Seelie Court. Now state your business, you've not long before the bridge closes."

I looked around in confusion. There was no bridge I could see, nor was there anyone else there but him.

"We need your help," Kaya butted in, approaching the mysterious stranger. "There is a Bòcan loose in Lochview."

"Why is that our problem?" The small man asked, folding his arms across his chest. "If you ask me, it couldn't happen to a more deserving place."

"What's wrong with Lochview?" I stepped forward strongly. We'd come for help, there was no need for him to be so rude.

"Lochview was our home," he said angrily. "That was until your precious Dowell family drove us away. For centuries we'd lived in harmony with humanity. Then all of a sudden, we are the enemy. You called us monsters and creatures. Treated us like wild animals."

His purple eyes glowed menacingly.

A cold chill ran down my back as a wave of chattering voices came from the trees around us.

"That must have been hundreds of years ago," Absy argued. "You can't blame us for what they did back then."

"In the coming days there is a festival that will be held in Lochview," the creature said bitterly. "A festival celebrating the day you drove the Fae out of Lochview."

He stepped towards us. His jaw clenched tight.

"So tell me, how are you any different?"

I turned to Archie. This couldn't be right. The Dowells protected Lochview, they wouldn't have turned on the innocent. They just wouldn't.

He looked down at his feet.

I felt sick.

My own ancestors had driven these people from their homes. It was my family's fault they hated humans.

"We're not different," I said. "We can still be cruel, and rude, and selfish. In fact, if you'd spoken to me a week ago, I'd have told you I didn't even believe in Fairies."

An angry grumble murmured from the trees.

"Sorry, I mean Fae," I quickly apologised. "We might be the same stupid Humans, but that doesn't mean we can't learn to be better."

The small man looked at me, unimpressed and unconvinced.

"Please, you're our only hope," I sighed. "If you don't help us, then Cináed will take Absy's soul, and I'll never see my family again."

The murmuring stopped suddenly.

"Say that name again," said the Fae before me, his eyes narrowing.

"Cináed?" I looked around sheepishly, unsure of what it'd done.

There was a moment of silence. I'm sure it was only a couple of seconds, but it felt like a lifetime.

"Tell me exactly what happened," he said finally, "and make it quick."

A wave of relief flooded through my body. My mouth started moving a million miles a minute as I told him every little detail, no matter how small. Absy tried to lie and say he found the coin, but Kaya's disapproving glare very quickly put an end to that.

"May I see the coin?" the Fae asked, as I came to the end of my story.

I rummaged in my pocket, pulling it out.

"It's broken," I said. "Cináed said it's run out of wishes."

"He is correct," the Fae said bluntly, "but that does not mean it is broken."

"You're saying it's just empty?" Kaya asked.

"Precisely," he replied.

"So, we just need to refill it," Absy asked.

The small man made an awkward face.

"It is not quite that simple," he said. "What you need to understand is that the soul of any living creature is immensely powerful. That token you hold in your hand traps a soul preventing it from leaving this plane of existence. The power can then be manifested in whatever way its owner desires. It is a very old magic. A very dark magic."

He shifted nervously on the spot.

All around us, there were frantic whispers and mutterings.

"But we found this in a whole chest of coins," Kaya pointed out. "Does that mean—"

"Like I said," he replied. "It is very old magic, and it is *very* dark magic."

"We read that there might be a way to trap him," Archie said, getting us back on track. "But we need to find a gateway to your world."

He turned and looked at his surroundings.

"Though perhaps we have already done that."

Suddenly there were angry and panicked voices coming from all around us.

"Silence!" the Fae in front of us shouted, his voice seemed to echo for miles. He turned back to Archie. "If you bring Cináed here, it could be very dangerous for us. To bring a Bòcan into the Seelie Court puts each and every one of us at risk. However, I also understand there may be no other way. This will have to be referred to the court."

As he stood pondering, a thin band of bright light burst down from above, creating a tiny dot in the centre of the circle.

"I'm afraid our time has come to an end," he said. "You will have our answer by nightfall."

The light began to spread, growing wider by the second until it filled the entire circle. A familiar buzzing started to build in my ears.

"But wait," I called back. "What about my family? How do I get them back?"

I only caught two words before the dark forest vanished and we landed back in the real world with a thud. But they were two words that squashed what little hope I had left.

I'm sorry.

22

"This is a waste of time," I growled, kicking out at one of the stones.

I was angry. Like really, really angry.

Everything had built to this moment, everything had built to them helping me get my family back, and they couldn't. Either that, or they wouldn't.

They were cowards.

They'd rather sit, hiding away in their trees, than stand up to Cináed. Let's face it, if they didn't have the courage to show themselves to us, then how could they ever stand up to a Bòcan?

But there was one realisation more painful than the rest.

If *they* couldn't stand up to a Bòcan, then what hope did we have?

I started walking.

I didn't know where I was going, I just knew I had to get away from there.

"Tyler, wait," Archie called after me.

I could hear his heavy footsteps as he jogged down the hill after me. Secretly, I wiped a tear from my eye as I felt his hand on my shoulder.

"Leave me alone." I couldn't turn around. I didn't want him to see me upset.

"Tyler, just stop!" His grip tightened, bringing me to a halt. "Look at me."

I shook my head.

I couldn't do it.

"Please, just turn around."

My eyes started to go blurry as I looked up at Archie's worried face.

"It's over," I said, my voice choking up. "They're gone and it's all my fault."

"Listen to me very carefully, young Master Tyler. It is not over until we have exhausted every possible option," he said firmly. "Whilst there is still breath in my body, I promise you, we will find another way."

A warmth spread through my chest. I was still terrified that my family were gone, but it was good to know I still had friends by my side.

"Tyler, are you OK?" Absy shouted.

He came marching down the hill with Kaya in tow.

"Yeah, I'm fine," I called back, rubbing my eyes. "I just got a bit frustrated."

"They might still help," Kaya said with a sympathetic smile. "And if they don't, we'll find a way to do it ourselves."

"Let's get back to the manor," Archie said, clapping

his hands. "I believe we are all long overdue a cup of tea."

Thankfully the walk downhill was much easier than the walk up. A short drive later and we were pulling through the gates of Lochview Manor.

The bright sunshine of the morning had given way to a sheet of dull grey clouds. There was a sudden chill in the air and it made me uncomfortable.

Something's wrong.

I didn't know what it was, but something felt off. As we came to a stop I took a quick look around, but there was nothing out of place.

I thought it was just my mind playing tricks on me.

But then we reached the front door.

"Archie, did you lock the door when we left?" Kaya asked nervously.

"Yes," he answered coming up the steps behind us. "Why?"

"Because it's not locked anymore."

We all stood frozen to the spot, staring at the heavy wooden door sitting ever so slightly ajar.

"Wait out here," Archie said, gripping the heavy iron handle.

"Not a chance," Absy replied. "If there is something dangerous here, then we should stick together. What if it takes us while you're inside?"

I looked disapprovingly at Absy, but he did have a point. There was no sense in splitting up.

"Very well, but stay close."

The door gently creaked open, echoing through the empty manor. We crept slowly across the black and white tiled floor. I went for the light switch, but Archie stopped me.

With a shake of his head, he pressed his finger to his lips.

As far as I could see, everything was exactly as we had left it.

Other than the door being open, there was no sign at all that anyone else had been there.

Archie stopped and took a deep breath.

"Is anyone there?" he bellowed.

We all stood in silence, listening for even the slightest sound.

Nothing.

"Maybe they've gone," Absy whispered.

Creak!

A chill ran up my spine.

"Or maybe they haven't," he whimpered.

Cautiously, we made our way down the corridor. Ahead we could see the door to the study lying open just a crack.

I could feel my heart thumping in my chest. With every step I took it beat faster and faster. Whoever, or whatever, had broken into the manor was waiting behind that door.

I held my breath as Archie reached for the handle. Time seemed to slow as he opened the door and revealed what lay beyond.

The room was trashed. Loose papers and books covered the floor and the desk, blowing in the breeze from the open window. Almost every inch of the room was covered by some kind of document.

Once the initial shock had passed, I let out a sigh of relief.

It was a mess, but at least we were alone.

"What is all this?" Absy asked.

"Just some old paperwork," Archie replied, hurriedly grabbing at the loose sheets. "Nothing of too much importance."

"Maybe they were looking for something?" Kaya suggested, picking up an open folder.

"Or maybe they just wanted to leave a message," I said.

Little did I know how right I was.

In the middle of the desk, I spotted something unusual. There was a letter lying separate from all the other scattered pieces of paper. Though it didn't say his name, I was fairly certain it was meant for Absy.

Dear Thief,

Firstly, I must commend you and your accomplices for seeking the help of the Seelie Court. I must regret to inform you, however, that it will be to no avail. They have neither the power nor the inclination to stand against me. Instead they will continue to cower away in their forgotten forests, just as they have always done.

Watching you all scurry around like lost little rats

*has been most entertaining, but it is now time to move
into the final act. You will soon be betrayed, and it will
be oh-so delicious. Even now the realisation must be
starting to dawn. The thought of what happens next.
There is a deal on the table that is still yet to be
discussed, and believe me, it has crossed your friend's
mind.*

I will have my payment, one way or another.

The waiting simply makes it all the sweeter.

"It's from *him*," I said, showing it to the others.
"Cináed was here."

"What does it mean?" Absy asked. "What deal is
on the table?"

I could feel Archie's eyes on me.

"I don't know," I said.

But it was a lie.

I knew what deal he was offering.

And it *had* already crossed my mind.

23

Whilst waiting for word from the Seelie Court, Kaya, Absy and I attempted to decipher the journal of Eustace Dowell. It was a long shot, but we hoped there was some clue we'd missed before, some other way to defeat Cináed.

Archie meanwhile set to work tidying the study. We did offer to help, but he insisted rather firmly that we should leave it to him.

Although we tried our best to concentrate on the dust-ridden book in front of us, it was obvious we were all distracted. We'd been sat for almost thirty minutes and yet had barely made it through four pages. I was starting to think Kaya had only turned the page to keep up the pretence.

Waiting for the Court felt like a waste of time, and I'm sure I wasn't the only one who thought it. We had no idea how or when they would make contact, nor did we know what their message would say.

Though I was fairly certain I could guess.

Cináed's words kept echoing around and around in my head, and I had to admit, he was right. Even if the Court were brave enough to stand against him, they had no reason to. Humans took their home from them, we took their lives from them, so why would they ever fight for us?

It was simple.

We had made this mess, we had to fix it.

Just like I had lost my family, so it was up to me to get them back.

Whatever it took.

"Iron!" Absy exclaimed, pointing excitedly at the bottom of the page. "It says here that even the slightest touch of iron can burn a Fae."

"The dust in my necklace," Kaya said, grasping at the locket. "It must have been some kind of iron powder."

"Well, could we get more?" Absy asked. "If a little bit will burn him, then maybe a lot will like melt him or something."

"I wouldn't even know where to find it." Kaya sat back, defeated.

"Archie might know," Absy replied. "What do you think, Tyler?"

"Yeah, maybe." The question caught me a little off guard.

"Tyler, are you alright?" Kaya asked.

"Yeah, I'm fine," I replied, giving myself a shake.

"You seem very quiet." There was a concerned

look in her eyes.

"I was just thinking about everything," I said, forcing a smile. "Honestly, I'm fine."

That was a lie.

The more the two of them talked, the more I worried. I was beginning to see how impossible my situation was. We were sat here finding ways to defeat Cináed, and I had no doubt that was the right thing to do. But stopping Cináed meant stopping the only person that knew how to bring my family back. If any of this worked, I'd lose them forever.

I slammed the book shut.

"It's getting late," I said bluntly. "Maybe we should start on all this again tomorrow."

"It's not even four o'clock," Absy replied, confused.

"Tyler, what's going on?" Kaya was starting to look really worried now.

"Nothing!" I rose from the sofa and started pacing by the fire. "I just think that maybe we should wait until we hear from the Court. We're sitting here planning, when they might fix it all for us. Besides, your parents will get suspicious if you get back too late. What if they work out that you didn't go to school?"

They exchanged a look.

"OK," Kaya said calmly. "You're right, we should get going."

Absy opened his mouth to argue but Kaya's glare stopped him.

"Are you going to school tomorrow?" She asked.

"Yeah, I think so," I replied. "I'm don't think Archie will call in sick for me again."

"We'll see you there then." She gave a smile and headed for the door. "Let us know if you hear anything."

"I will."

Just as they were about to step into the hallway, Kaya stopped.

"And, Tyler," she said, "if you need anyone to talk to, you know we're here for you, right? Whatever happens, we've got your back."

I felt a pang of guilt as they left. Maybe I was too harsh in the way I spoke to them, but I couldn't let them come up with a plan that might put my family at risk.

"Where is everyone?"

I looked up to see Archie standing in the doorway.

"Absy and Kaya had to go," I lied. "Something about getting home before their parents."

"Yes," he said disapprovingly. "That is the trouble with deceit, it takes far more effort to maintain a lie than to tell the truth."

"Yeah, I guess so," I said quietly.

"Tyler, is everything OK?" Archie asked.

"I'm just tired," I replied. "I might go upstairs for a bit. It's been a long day."

I forced a small smile and he nodded gently.

"Very well, you head up and I shall give you a knock for dinner."

I thanked him and made my way to the stairs.

When I reached the bottom step, I stopped and looked back over my shoulder. Certain I was out of view, I turned around, grabbed my coat and snuck out through the front door. Hurrying as fast as my legs would carry me, I made my way towards town.

Inside I was a mess of fear and guilt, but I couldn't let it stop me. I tried to tell myself that I wasn't betraying my friends, but that was exactly what it felt like.

Deep down I knew they wouldn't understand.

There was only one person that could give me what I wanted.

One person that could bring my family back.

He just had to name his price.

24

Staring down at the door to The Beyond, I started to wonder if this was really such a good idea. Maybe it wasn't too late to turn back, maybe I should try speaking to the others.

Creak!

Before I had a chance to change my mind, the door opened. I craned my neck trying to look inside, but there was no one there. At least no one I could see. It was just darkness and shadows.

It felt like a trap, but I had no other choice.

Slowly, I descended the stairs, my legs trembling beneath me. When I got to the bottom, I took a deep breath, then I stepped inside.

The shop was empty, but not like full of shelves with nothing on empty. It was completely empty. There was nothing at all, just the bare wooden floor. It was so dark I couldn't even make out the walls.

"Tyler," said a voice. It almost seemed to echo from deep within the shadows. "I'm so glad you came."

I looked around, but there was no sign of anyone. Yet still the voice continued, filling every corner of the room.

"Please, do take a seat."

I felt a nudge at the back of my knees.

Out of nowhere a small wooden chair had appeared.

I glanced beyond it and my heart gave a thud.

The front door was gone. On all sides I was surrounded by the deepest blackness I'd ever seen.

"Tyler, sit."

My legs gave way and I landed in the chair. I could feel the panic rising in my chest. I tried to stand back up, but my body wouldn't respond.

"Don't fight it, just try to relax."

Cináed stepped forward into the dim light, baring his sharp teeth in a twisted smile.

"Let me go," I grunted, wrestling with my own body.

"All in good time," he said, his raspy voice lifting playfully. "First, I must be certain that you are not a threat. Why have you come here?"

With a heavy sigh, I stopped fighting.

"I want my family back," I said quietly, barely able to even look him in the eyes.

"Interesting," he grinned. "I trust you are darkening my door because the Seelie Court have proved as useless as ever. Tell me, how frightened were they to hear my name?"

"I'm not here to play games," I snapped. "Can you

help me or not?"

"The boy has bite!" He exclaimed, dancing around with glee and excitement. Mocking me at every turn. "It is certainly possible, but I would of course require something in return."

I had known this moment would come, but it didn't make me any less nervous.

"What do you want?"

"How very good of you to ask." He stepped forward. "Do you have my coin in your possession?"

I watched in horror as my hand reached into my pocket, retrieved the coin and held it out towards him.

"Perfect," he said. "You are going to use that coin to take your friend Abdirahman's soul for me."

"Why?" I asked, but his grin only widened.

"For my entertainment." He licked his lips menacingly. "I am going to watch and savour every precious moment of your torment."

"But why does it have to be me?" I managed to move slightly in the chair. In all his excitement, Cináed's grip was loosening. "Why not do it yourself? If you're this big powerful Bòcan, then why can't you do your own dirty work?"

Crash!

I burst free from the chair, sending it skidding across the floor. As I threw myself up onto my feet, I found myself nose to nose with Cináed.

His breath was warm and stale.

"Do not underestimate me, boy," he whispered. "I

could take what I am owed whenever I please, but where is the fun in that? Think how much more satisfying it would be to have you, his friend, betray him on my behalf. Now that is true power."

A cold shiver ran through my entire body.

He was right. He was pure evil, but he was right. I had no choice, it was Absy or my family.

"What do I have to do?"

He took the coin from my hand and held it in front of my face.

"Come noon tomorrow, when the sun is highest in the sky. You will take this, and you will clasp it in your friend's hand. Simply speak his name and it will be done."

"And you'll bring back my family."

"You have my word."

He held out the coin towards me.

I hesitated for a moment, but there was nothing else I could do. This was how it had to be.

Crack!

As my fingers touched the cold metal, a snap of electricity ripped through the air. All of a sudden, I was back in The Beyond. The door lay open behind me, just as I had left it. Outside it had started to rain.

For a brief moment, I stood motionless. My chest heaved as I tried to catch my breath.

Everything suddenly felt very real. The wheels were in motion, there was nothing I could do to stop them.

Pulling my coat tightly around me, I stepped

outside. It wasn't the heaviest of rain, but it was enough to soak you through. I ducked my head as I quickly ran up the stairs.

As I reached the top I came to an abrupt stop. In the alleyway ahead stood a darkened figure waiting in the shadows.

"I think you and I need to talk, Master Tyler."

Archie looked at me disappointedly from underneath his umbrella.

"I'm sorry, Archie," I replied. "I didn't have a choice."

"The Seelie Court made contact," he continued. "It was really rather clever. They had written it on a window, but it only appeared when there was condensation on the glass. I started boiling potatoes for dinner and then suddenly there it was."

I tried to speak, but he barely paused for breath.

"We are to meet them tomorrow," he said. "Or at least, they have requested we meet them tomorrow. I suppose whether or not we go is up to you."

The guilt was overwhelming. The way he was looking at me was like a dagger in my gut.

"Archie, I need you to trust me," I pleaded. "I know what I'm doing."

"And what is that?" he asked bluntly.

"I can't tell you."

I really couldn't. I had no idea how much Cináed could see and hear. After all, he knew we'd been to the Seelie Court. He knew he could find us back at the Manor. He was always one step ahead.

So for now, I needed Archie to have faith in me. I needed him to believe that I would do the right thing.

"I can fix this," I said, summoning all the confidence I could muster. "I promise you, I can fix all of this."

25

There was no room for error.

I knew that Cináed would be watching my every move. If he thought, even for a second, I was turning against him, then my family were toast.

From the moment I woke up, I was terrified. Even the tiniest things, like getting ready for school, had my palms sweating. It took me four attempts just to tie my tie.

Staring in the mirror, I kept imagining the scene. I pictured Absy meeting me at the school gates, completely ignorant of what was about to happen. Cináed watching on as I grasped his hand.

There was a knock at the door.

"Master Tyler, are you coming down for breakfast?" Archie called from the hallway.

"Yeah, I'll be down in a minute," I replied.

As I heard his footsteps fade I took a deep breath.

It was time for the first test of the day.

After making my way downstairs, I took a seat

opposite him at the kitchen table. Despite my attempt to play it cool, to pretend that nothing was going on, I could feel his eyes watching me. A couple of times he tried to start a conversation, but I never answered with more than a grunt or a nod. Eventually he gave up.

"Well then," he said with a defeated sigh. "I supposed we better get you to school."

I can't begin to explain how much I wanted to talk, how much I wanted to tell him exactly what was going on, but I stayed strong. If I told him, he would try to stop me. I wasn't going to let that happen. No, I couldn't let that happen.

Instead, I waited until his back was turned and slipped a folded piece of paper under the fruit bowl. On it I explained everything, what I was about to do and why. He deserved to know, but at least this way I knew it would be too late to get in my way.

With my letter planted, I grabbed my bag and headed for the front door.

The weather was grey and drizzly as Archie drove me to school. It felt kind of fitting. Depressing weather, for a depressing day.

Outside the school, the usual sea of green blazers had been replaced by a mix of heavy coats. Everyone filed through the gates with their hoods up and their heads down, rushing to get inside to the warm.

Everyone that was except for two stragglers stood hovering by the wall. I saw Kaya look up as Archie brought the car to a halt.

I reached for the handle, but he stopped me.

"Tyler, whatever is going on, just remember we are here to help," he said. "If you need me, you only have to ask."

Little did he know just how much I needed him, just how much I needed all of them. I was desperate to speak, but instead I just thanked him and stepped out into the rain.

Kaya and Absy rushed over to me.

"Did you hear from the Court?" Absy asked, with all the subtlety of a brick.

"They're not going to help," I lied.

Disappointment washed over their faces.

"But don't worry," I said. "I've got a plan."

"What is it?" Kaya whispered, glancing cautiously over her shoulder.

"Not now." I shook my head. "I'll explain later. For now, just make sure that when the lunch bell rings, you get to this exact spot as quickly as you can."

They both nodded. I could see a glimmer of hope in their eyes, but all it did was add to the knot that was twisting around in my gut. I had a feeling they wouldn't be looking at me the same way come lunchtime.

"We better get to class," I said.

I was trying to act like nothing was wrong, but as we crossed the playground my eyes kept darting through the crowd. I was checking every corner, every window, every shadow. I knew Cináed would be watching. I just didn't know from where.

The warm air hit me instantly as we made our way through the front doors. The rustle of coats and umbrellas filled the hallway. Accompanied by the chatting and shouting of people making their way to class.

Yet despite all the noise, a single voice cut through.

"Decided to join us today then?"

We turned to find Mrs Allen standing, arms crossed, in the middle of the corridor.

"Yes, Miss," Absy replied. "We were all a bit under the weather yesterday, but we're feeling better now."

"Well, that is very good to hear," she said. "I shall expect your company for detention at lunchtime then."

"What? No!" I cried.

"No?" she repeated, raising her eyebrows.

"You can't give us detention," I argued. "We've not done anything wrong."

"I'm not sure how things were done at your previous school, Mr Buckland," she replied sharply. "But when I send you to the headteacher's office, I expect you to wait to be seen by the headteacher."

A rush of panic raced through my veins.

This was more than just a blip.

This could ruin everything.

"We're sorry, Miss," Kaya said, as I stood frozen to the spot.

"As you very well should be," she replied. "I'll see the three of you in my classroom at twelve."

26

Inevitable.

That was the only word for it.

Twelve o'clock was approaching fast, like a meteor set to wipe out planet Earth. With every second that ticked by my heart raced a little bit faster.

I was sitting in Mrs Allen's English class, watching the clock. There was only a matter of minutes until the bell would ring. Then everyone would file out, laughing and cheering as they rushed out into the hall, and we'd be left alone.

That was when it would happen.

That was when it had to happen.

I glanced out the window.

Where is Cináed?

I knew he'd want to make a grand entrance, that much was obvious. I just didn't know how or when he'd appear. The thought alone was enough to put me on edge.

A girl at the front of the class dropped her pen and I nearly leapt out my skin.

Kaya nudged me in the side.

"Are you OK?" she whispered.

No, I was the farthest possible thing from OK. Knowing what was coming next, how could I be?

Not that I could tell her that.

Ring!

My heart sank.

It was time. In a chaotic flurry of movement everyone packed up their things and grabbed their bags. Hidden amongst the commotion I seized my chance.

"Kaya, I need you to listen to me very carefully," I said grabbing her by the hand.

"OK," she replied, her face a mix of shock and confusion.

"Whatever happens next, I need you to trust me." People were starting to move towards the door. I didn't have much time. "You won't want to, but please, it's the only way."

Quickly, I took my book and tucked it away in my backpack.

Kaya just sat staring at me, her eyes wide.

"Tyler and Kaya, you can stay where you are," Mrs Allen said, wiping the whiteboard clean. "I'm sure Abdirahman will be along to join us soon."

I felt sick.

We shouldn't be here.

We should be outside, I planned it to be outside.

Looking out beyond the school's iron gates, I saw a familiar sight.

I felt a dull thud in my chest.

It was Archie's car.

Knock, knock!

I turned to the door to see Absy walk in apologetically.

"Sorry, I'm late."

"Actually, you are right on time," Mrs Allen replied, in a strangely jubilant tone. "Before you sit down could you grab me a workbook from the cupboard?"

"Sure." He looked at us with a confused expression.

Why was she acting so weird?

When he reached the cupboard at the back of the classroom, he pulled the handle and then stopped.

"Tyler, Kaya, you guys should see this."

We looked up at Mrs Allen, but she didn't even turn around. It was like she hadn't heard him. Either that or she was ignoring him. Slowly, we climbed to our feet and made our way over to Absy. A small gasp escaped Kaya's lips as we peered over his shoulder.

Suddenly it all made sense.

Mrs Allen wasn't ignoring him.

She couldn't be.

Mrs Allen was lying unconscious in the stationary cupboard.

27

"It's him!" Absy cried.

Buzz!

The imposter's eyes began to glow a deep purple as the tingle of static electricity flooded through the room. Our English teacher's body started to stretch and contort in front of us. I watched in horror as her limbs twisted and turned until she had been replaced entirely by the grey-faced Bòcan.

"Well, isn't this lovely," he said, with a sharp-toothed smile. "All of us together once again. It really is a shame it can't stay that way."

"Don't come any closer," Absy shouted, backing away slowly.

"Oh, don't you worry," Cináed grinned. "I have no intention of coming anywhere near you."

"Then what do you want?" Kaya asked.

"I am here to collect what I am owed," he said simply.

"Well, you can't have it," Absy bit back. "I'm not giving you my soul."

"I'm afraid you should have thought of that before stealing my property," he shrugged.

"It was a mistake," Absy argued. "I didn't know what it was, I just thought it looked cool. Please, if I could go back, then I never would have taken it."

"But you can't go back," he replied. "You took something that wasn't yours and now you must pay the price."

"What if we were to offer you something else?" Kaya interrupted desperately.

Cináed stopped.

"I'm listening." A wry smile crossed his lips. "What did you have in mind?"

"What do you want?" she asked, her voice trembling.

"That is a very broad question." He stepped towards her. "I'm far more interested in what you are willing to give. What value would you put on your friend's soul?"

"I don't know," Kaya stuttered, tears forming in her eyes.

"It's OK," the Bòcan whispered gently, placing a hand on her shoulder. "In truth, I am afraid there is nothing you can offer that would save your friend. You are quite simply too late."

"What do you mean?" Kaya asked nervously.

"Someone else got there before you." Cináed let

out an evil chuckle as he stepped away from Kaya. "I am sorry, children, but there is a traitor in your midst."

I felt both Kaya and Absy's eyes turn to me.

"Tyler, what's going on?" Absy said, terror in his eyes.

"I'm sorry, Absy."

I wanted to throw up.

I watched as a look of fear spread across his face. It was unbearable. A tidal wave of guilt hit me like a punch in the gut. But I couldn't stop. I had to finish this.

Slowly I walked towards him, reaching into my pocket for the coin.

"It's the only way," I said, trying to explain. "He said he can bring my family back, but this is the price. I'm so sorry."

Then he said the words that nearly made me fall apart. Five words that nearly broke me.

"I thought we were friends."

I couldn't look him in the eye. It took everything I had to just keep putting one foot in front of the other. I knew it had to be like this, but there was no way I could have possibly imagined it was going to be this hard.

"It's not going to hurt," I promised. "I just hold the coin against your hand, say your name, and then it's over. It's as simple as that."

"Less talk, Tyler," Cináed demanded. "If you want to see your family again, you know what you must do."

I could see the excitement building in his eyes. He licked his lips as he savoured every moment.

"You promise?" I asked.

"My word is my bond."

I took a deep breath and reached out towards Absy.

He tried to pull away, but I locked him in a firm grip.

"I'm so sorry," I whispered.

"Please don't do this," he begged.

I held his hand tight.

I looked him dead in the eye.

Then I winked.

"Kaya, now!" I cried.

Before Cináed had even a second to react, Kaya grabbed his hand and pressed the coin tight against his skin.

"Consider the debt paid," she said with a smile, before bellowing his name at the top of her lungs. "Cináed!"

His eyes opened wide with terror.

"No!" he cried, as his skin began to crack and fizz.

His mouth twisted into a silent scream as the coin began to smoke in his palm. A blinding light burst from within him, filling the room.

I shielded my eyes as it built and built, getting brighter and brighter. For a moment I worried that it would burn us up to.

Suddenly it stopped. The noise, the light, everything was gone.

Clink!

It took a moment for my eyes to adjust. When they did, I found the classroom completely undisturbed. There was not a single sign of what had happened. No evidence of anything at all.

Except for one small detail.

In the exact spot where Cináed had stood, now lay a shiny gold coin.

28

The classroom door burst open. On the other side stood Archie, out of breath, with a thick iron chain in his hands.

"Is everyone OK?" he cried, panting heavily.

"We're fine," I replied. "He's gone."

Satisfied that we were safe, his panic very quickly turned to anger.

"You said you'd be at the gates at noon," he said. "Where were you?"

"Things changed." I looked at him apologetically. "We had to think on our feet."

It was clear that Archie wasn't happy, but at least we were all still here.

"Absy, are you OK?" Kaya asked.

In all the commotion, I'd almost forgotten he was there.

He stood frozen, staring directly at me. His face was a mixture of shock and confusion. His mouth moved, but he was struggling to find his words.

"You were going to give him my soul," he said finally.

"Absy, maybe you should sit down." I reached out, but he stepped away.

"No. He said you made a deal. He said you were working for him." He bumped into a table trying to keep a distance between us.

"It was all part of the plan Absy, I promise." There was a familiar sense of guilt in the pit of my stomach. "I knew he would be watching so I had to keep it all a secret. I couldn't say anything, but believe me, I really wished I could."

"That's why you told us to meet you at the gates," Kaya realised.

"I left Archie a note this morning," I explained. "I told him to wait by the gates with something iron that we could use to trap Cináed—"

"Then Mrs Allen gave us detention," she interrupted.

"Exactly. Outside, we'd have had the space and the freedom to catch him off guard. Once we had him where we wanted him, I was going to force him to bring my family back and then trap him with the coin," I paused. "But in here it was too much of a risk. Without Archie or any kind of weapon, he had the advantage, so I had to improvise. I had to find a way to protect Absy at all costs. I knew his eyes would be on me, that's why I snuck the coin to you when the bell went."

"Very clever, Master Tyler," Archie said proudly. "Very clever indeed."

"What about your family?" Absy asked quietly.

I hesitated.

It was the one question I didn't want to think about.

Cináed was the only one with the power to bring them back, and now he was gone. Not only was it my fault they disappeared in the first place, but now I'd thrown away their only hope of coming back.

I could feel them all looking at me.

"I don't know," I replied, and that was the most honest answer I could give.

"You sacrificed them for me." I could see Absy's eyes glistening as he fought back tears. "I'm so sorry."

"It's OK." I sat back against the table. "I'll try speaking to the Seelie Court again. Maybe there is something they can do."

"But I thought they weren't going to help us?" Kaya asked.

"Well, that's not strictly true." I shrugged awkwardly. "They wanted to speak to us again, but by the time they responded I'd already gone rogue."

Absy shook his head.

"No, they said they couldn't help," he pointed out.

"It might still be worth a try." I knew I was clutching at straws, but it was all I had left.

"Or maybe there is another way." He jumped to his feet and marched towards the spot where Cináed had been standing.

"Absy, what are you doing?" I asked nervously as he crouched down and picked up the coin. "That thing has done enough damage already."

"You were willing to sacrifice your family for me, I think I owe you," he said with a smile. "Besides, I'm sure one more wish can't hurt."

He wrapped his fingers tightly around the coin and closed his eyes.

"I wish Tyler had his family back."

It felt like there should have been some big dramatic moment. Some kind of explosion or a burst of flames.

But there was nothing.

Just Absy stood perfectly still whilst we all watched in anticipation.

"Did it work?" he asked, opening one eye.

"I don't know," I replied.

Buzz!

My heart stopped, but it was just my phone vibrating in my pocket.

I had a new message.

A message from Dad.

What do you want for dinner? Your mum says she'll pick you up from school today and is going to pop to the shop on the way.

Pure joy spread through my body. I couldn't find the words to speak so I just wrapped my arms around Absy.

They were back. He'd brought them back.

"Alright, calm down," he laughed, breaking away from me. "I think we can call that even."

He held out his hand.

"Even," I agreed, giving it a firm shake.

Absy held up the coin.

"You know this thing is still pretty golden," he said. "Maybe it's got a couple more wishes in it."

"Not a chance." Kaya snatched it from his grip and placed it safely in her pocket.

"Party pooper," he teased with a grin.

A noise from behind us cut the celebrations short.

"Archie, you better go," I said, glancing over my shoulder.

"Why what's going on?" he asked.

The noise repeated, but this time louder.

"Tyler's right." Kaya started shepherding him towards the door. "We'll speak to you later."

"I'm not going anywhere until you tell me what that noise is," Archie demanded, putting his foot down.

Groan!

I gave a defeated sigh.

"I think Mrs Allen is waking up."

29

Luckily for us, Mrs Allen didn't remember how she came to be in the cupboard. In fact, she didn't remember much of anything, including giving us detention that morning. Instead, she thanked us for helping her and told us we were free to go.

The afternoon sailed by, and before I knew it the bell was ringing. I could barely contain my excitement as I joined the stampede of students flooding out towards the gates. Kaya kept laughing at me, but all I could do was smile.

We'd done it.

We'd actually done it.

We'd defeated Cináed and we'd brought my family back.

All was right with the world once again.

I can't even begin to describe the mix of relief and joy I felt when I saw Mum's car parked by the road. I was about to go running towards her, but Kaya grabbed my arm and told me to play it cool.

She was right, obviously. If I seemed too excited to see her, then she'd know that someone was wrong.

Not that anything was wrong anymore.

It was over.

Well, it was nearly over.

There was one last thing we had to do before we could lay all this to rest.

We all agreed that after everything we'd seen, it wouldn't be right for us to celebrate the Rowan Festival. At least not in the way that everyone else was.

So, whilst the rest of Lochview lined the streets partying and cheering, Kaya, Absy and I took a trip up to Seelie Point. Despite everything that had happened in the past, the court still offered to help when we needed them. To us, that felt like a much more worthwhile thing to celebrate.

Plus, we had something that we thought might be a little safer with them.

Though not everyone was totally sold on the idea.

"Just one more wish," Absy begged as Kaya placed the coin in the centre of the circle.

"For the last time, no!" she replied firmly. "It uses Fae magic, so it should be with the Fae."

The sun was high in the sky and there were only a few seconds until noon. Kaya stepped back out of the circle. We all stood watching, waiting for something to happen.

"And that's twelve," I announced, staring at my watch.

At first, nothing happened.

Then slowly the ground beneath the coin seemed to soften, swallowing it down into the earth.

"It's sinking," Absy said.

Me and Kaya grabbed him as he almost stepped inside the circle.

In a matter of seconds, it was gone. The last trace of Cináed and everything that had happened. It was like a massive weight had been lifted off my shoulders.

We decided to sit a while at the top of the hill before making the long walk back down. From Seelie Point you could see for miles, almost to the far banks of Loch Dowell. The manor was practically a dot on its shores.

Everything was so peaceful and quiet.

That was until Absy started rummaging in his bag for his packet of crisps.

It felt good to know I had friends like them, friends that would always have my back. Yet still there was something playing on my mind.

Friends shouldn't have secrets.

"There's something I need to tell the two of you," I said.

"OK," Kaya replied, a little surprised.

"It's something about me." I took a deep breath. "Something I didn't even know myself until I moved here. Though really, it was actually Archie that discovered it—"

"Tyler, we know," Absy mumbled around a mouth full of crisps.

It was my turn to be surprised.

"You know?" I repeated.

"Of course we do," he shrugged. "Hanging around with Archie, spending all that time in the Manor, not to mention all the weird monster stuff. It's pretty obvious."

I didn't know what to say, I just stared at him in amazement.

Suddenly he burst out laughing.

"Don't listen to him," Kaya grinned. "We saw your family tree when the study got trashed. It must have fallen out of one of the folders."

"It must be pretty cool though, the Dowells are like royalty," Absy said.

"They're nobility," Kaya corrected.

"Whatever, either way they must be pretty rich," he continued, turning back to me. "And what about the Manor. If they're your long-lost relatives, does that make it yours?"

"According to Archie, it doesn't work that way," I said, but deep down I really wish it did.

"You know, I reckon there are probably plenty of other weird things lurking in Lochview," he pondered. "The town probably needs someone to help protect it."

"And who did you have in mind?" Kaya said with a hint of a smile.

144

"Well, I don't see any other Dowells around," he pointed out. "Though naturally he would need a couple of good friends at his side."

"Well obviously," Kaya agreed. "But where could he possibly find two awesome people that would be happy to help him?"

They both started scratching their chins, pretending to think.

"I don't suppose the two of you would be interested?" I replied, playing their game.

They both smiled.

"We thought you'd never ask."

And that was how it began.

Three friends ready to stand against whatever might come our way.

Kaya, Absy and Tyler, the protectors of Lochview.

Tyler Buckland returns in
House of the Claw

Ready For More?

Scan below to keep up to date
with all things Lochview!

Made in the USA
Las Vegas, NV
08 December 2023